Diamonds Aren't for Everyone

Triplets: Three Aren't One

Book Two

by

Dani Haviland

USA Today Bestselling Author

Copyright

Book Description

Birthday mayhem turns into a hunt for her parents' blackmailers. Will a rich heir ruin Vickie's plans?

Praise and Awards

"There wasn't a heartstring this one didn't pull at! And, no spoilers, but that's one of the nicest endings I could have imagined – all round, proving redemption's possible, some things will last forever, and …. Karma. This isn't just a story of Jose and Loren; it's so much more.   Amazon reader on *Too Fast for You* (http://bit.ly/2fast4YOU)

"From the picturesque descriptions of the Alaskan wilderness, to weaving a beautiful love story, the author's writing style is both serious and quirky. A perfect, relaxing read!"
  Amazon review of *One Arctic Summer* (http://bit.ly/2OneArcticSummer)

Chapter 1: New Old Parents

January 3, 1992

"Is anyone following us?" Gloria asked, checking the side mirror of their Cadillac.

"Why would they be? We didn't do anything wrong," her husband said, now worried too.

"Other than adopt a baby without papers or even the birthmother's okay."

"First off…" Roger paused a moment to collect his wits and recheck the rearview mirror, then started again. "I seriously doubt that birth mothers are ever around when their babies are adopted out. Plus, I don't think Dr. Buddy would have let all three of her babies go without getting her permission."

"Dr. Buddy lied to us, though," she said. "Remember? Maybe he tricked the mother and lied to her, too. Imagine, getting over $80,000 from us upfront for his fee and expenses, and then telling us the mother and babies had died. I'm so glad Chuck came to our rescue. I only met him a couple of times, but I don't think he'd steal three babies from a mother who wanted them. She must have been overwhelmed. I mean, really? Can you imagine how daunting it would be to raise three babies all at once?"

"I watched my sister with just one at a time," Roger said. "No, I can't imagine twins, much less triplets. There must be more to the story. I have the feeling that Chuck knows more about what's going on but he's sparing us."

"So, do you think people will really believe I'm her natural mother?" Gloria asked, pulling down the visor to examine the faint crow's feet at the corners of her eyes.

"My dear wife, you're only forty years old. Lots of women your age give birth. More than anything, they'll wonder how you got your figure back so soon. Or even how you hid a pregnancy so well. You're as much a fox now as you were twenty years ago."

"Well, I'll simply say I didn't want to announce the pregnancy, just in case something went wrong. Of course, since the baby is so small, I can say that's why I recovered my shape so quickly." Gloria flipped the mirror up out of the way, then pulled the zipper down on her ski jacket to look inside at the face of her newborn treasure again. "She is so beautiful..."

"Yes, she is," Roger agreed. "Let's cancel all our social engagements for the next month or two. I want to spend as much time with her as..."

"But...but..."

"No buts. Hear me out. If we're off everyone's radar for a while, we can say we've been taking care of our new addition. That will be the truth, won't it?"

"Well, the two of us plus the nanny..."

"Fine. With or without the nanny, we'll make sure we get lots of pictures of us which should help support our absence. I think it's ridiculous to pretend she's our natural child, but if that's what you really want to do," Roger said, then sighed. "Nobody needs to know whether the adoption was through an agency or out the side door of a converted utility van. And before you ask for the seventh time in ten minutes, you're plenty young enough to have a child. If only those fertility shots had worked for you."

"They made us both crazy. Or rather, they made me over the hills hormonal and irrational and that almost drove you crazy. I didn't want to risk losing you because of it."

"Well, those *were* four very emotionally charged months," Roger agreed, recalling the screaming, crying, and knife-throwing episodes.

"How many times am I going to have to apologize..." Grace began, then stopped when she saw his head shaking. "Oh, you weren't looking for an apology."

"Let's move forward, shall we? Just you and me and baby makes three. Are you sure you want to name her Victoria, though?"

"Victoria like my sister? Heavens, no!" Gloria exclaimed, startling the baby snuggled next to her.

She brought her voice down and soothed the hours-old baby she had disturbed, "There, there, Vickie Lynn. You'll be home to a nice warm bottle in about three minutes. Mommy's here for you."

Roger glanced over at the two of them and grinned. Content. Happier now than he ever thought possible. "I'm glad to hear you call yourself Mommy. Mother sounds so stilted and formal. I never could understand why *she* insisted Grace call her Mother. Her own, biological daughter… That sounds so stoic and sterile."

"Grrr," Gloria groaned. "*She's* the reason I hate the name Victoria so much. The name on her birth certificate read Vickie but she hated it. 'Vickie' is such a common name,' she argued. 'It really should be Victoria. I'm like a queen – I'll be remembered long after I'm gone.' She whined so much about it that Dad changed it legally to Victoria for her twelfth birthday. I think it may have been part of the reason our mom had a heart attack. She loved her Grandma Vickie so much that it was an emotional slap in the face to just throw out the name like that. You couldn't prove to me that Victoria didn't agitate her on purpose with stunts like that. She knew Mom had a weak heart. Damn *Victoria* still!" she said with disdain.

"You won't hear me argue that one," Roger said. "I lost my favorite cousin and best friend in the whole world because of her, but as I was just saying, we have a fresh start, right?"

Gloria reached up and patted her husband on the shoulder. "You may have been second in line for my hand, but you were and still are the best man for me, Roger Stillwater Thornwhistle."

"And you for me, Gloria Lynn Thornwhistle."

***

"Oh, dear," Gloria fretted, pacing back and forth, trying to soothe the squalling baby. "I think I need to call the nanny right now. Something's wrong. She won't quit crying."

3

"Hold on a sec," Roger said patiently, holding back his frustration. One of them losing it was one too many.

Ding!

Roger took the bottle of water out of the microwave, stirred in the suggested amount of formula, swirled it around, and then capped the bottle.

"Here," Gloria said, grabbing for it.

"Nope," he said, pulling it away. He tipped a small amount of formula on the inside of his wrist, verifying the temperature, then handed it to her. "Perfect. Body temp."

Gloria snuggled Vickie close then clumsily tried to feed her the bottle. "Damn! I think I need my reading glasses just to find her mouth!"

The baby's mouth turned and latched onto the nipple that had struck her cheek, leaving a milky mess. Roger grabbed a tissue and wiped it clean. "Smart girl. She'll find the food. Just get it in the general area, but make sure it's not too hot or too cold."

"How did you know that?"

"I read up on it, plus I did hang out with my sister's sons every once in a while. Just keep her warm, dry, and well-fed and she'll soon be our little princess in satin and lace."

"She can be our princess in satin right now," Gloria said, "but lace will have to wait until her skin isn't so tender. See. I hung out with your sister a bit, too."

***

Two weeks before Christmas, 1995
Nearly four years later

"Where'd she go?" Gloria asked in a panic.

"What do you mean, 'Where'd she go'?" Roger huffed. "I thought you had her!"

"I did! She said she was going to see you. I looked up, there you were, and now she's gone!"

"You go that way; I'll check over in the toys," Roger said. "I don't believe in tethers, but I wish I had her on one right now."

***

Near the carousel

"I remember when you were little," Hal said, his arm around Grace's shoulder. "I'd bring you here to ride the pink unicorn. No matter how long I let you ride, you'd always ask for 'one more turn.' It'd irritate your mother to no end if she was here with us, too."

"I think I remember that," Grace said. "She'd stomp her foot and walk away when you gave into me."

Hal chuckled at the memory but didn't add to the story.

"And if I remember right, you'd let me ride until I wet my pants."

"Hey, that wasn't my fault. You didn't tell me you had to go."

"Yeah, well, you should have known. When we'd come here, you'd let me have anything I wanted. I wonder if they still have those orange juice and ice cream milkshakes…"

"Here you go, Dad," Dusty said, handing Hal his 'orange-sicle' drink. "And I got the largest size they made for Grace."

"You remembered!" Grace said, accepting the giant cup.

"It's still good for you: juice and milk. Add a few bacon bits and strudel crumbles and you have all four food groups," Hal said, smiling.

Grace looked toward the carousel and blanched in horror. She clumsily set her cup down and rushed to the flimsy security fence, swooping up the little blonde, sparing the tyke a disastrous tumble into the twirling ride.

"Whoa there, honey," Grace soothed, holding her close. "You have to wait until it stops to get on."

"I want to ride the pink ooni-corn," Vickie said, reaching out.

"Okay. Let's wait for it to stop, and then I'll ride with you. Will that be all okay?"

Vickie looked up at Grace and squinted, studying her features, then back at the twirling ride that was slowing down.

"Again?"

5

"Well, for me it will be again," Grace said. She looked back at her dad and Dusty. "Call security and tell them they have a lost little girl at the carousel. Maybe they can find her parents."

Hal stared at the duo, frozen in shock at the resemblance of the little blonde beauty to Grace when she was that age. She could have been a pint-sized clone of her.

"Um, Dad? Do you want me to go tell them or do you want to?" Dusty asked. When Hal didn't respond, he said, "Okay. I'll go."

"This was my favorite when I was your age, too," Grace said, hoping she didn't scare the little girl. "How old are you?"

"Vickie Lynn."

Grace realized the girl was confused, so she tried the other oft-asked question. "What's your name?"

"I'm this many tomorrow," she said, holding up four fingers, using her other hand to keep her thumb from popping up.

"And what's your Mommy's name?"

"Vickie Lynn January Third."

The carousel came to a stop beside them. "Here's the unicorn," Grace said, hoisting her up. "This was my favorite one, too. So, is your name Vickie Lynn?"

The little girl in the pink satin coat trimmed with a real white fur clung to the bronze pole in the middle of her magical creature, rising up and down, oblivious of the questions trying to intrude on her quest to find the rest of the unicorns in fantasy land.

Grace put her interrogation on pause, letting the little girl enjoy the ride. Certainly, her parents would be found soon. Who would let someone so precious out of their sight? Then again, she'd never let anyone get in her way of riding the pink 'oonicorn' when she was that age, either. Tears welled in her eyes as she realized that her twins would have been this age if she had kept them. Why had she balked? Given up on them even before she let them know her? Maybe they wouldn't have died if she had had them in a hospital, not at Dr. Buddy's birthing center?

Her smile dropped as the reasons smacked her in the gut like

6

one-two punches. Those threats to Dusty and his father were why. Victoria – she refused to even think of her as Mother – was long gone now, a resident of Costa Rica thanks to Dad's not-too-subtle threat of blackmail. Dusty was back in her life – safe – and her husband for almost four years now. If she would have known that circumstances would be in her favor, she wouldn't have given up hope and the twins. No looking back on that now. Hopefully, the fertility specialist had a solution to her recent sterility and they could start anew with more children.

"Again! Again!" Vickie Lynn demanded, bouncing up and down.

"I got it," Hal called from below, nodding to the carousel operator who had been given a healthy tip to keep the ride going for the blonde pair clinging to the magical animal of fiberglass and pink resin.

Hal sighed at the beautiful blondes, so much like a mother and daughter in looks and favorite animals. *I wonder if the twins were girls? I know it shouldn't make a difference because they're dead, but it does. If I had only seen them for a moment, even an ultrasound of their little feet kicking, their little bodies twisting and turning, their little bottoms showing off which gender they were…*

"Oh, thank God!" Roger said, stopping short at the sight of his young daughter with a beautiful blonde supporting her on the carousel.

"I take it she's yours," Hal said, then blanched as he looked back and saw who was speaking. "Roger?"

"Hal?" Roger asked. He glanced back momentarily to verify the voice belonged to his cousin, then was focused back on Vickie. "It's been… Yes, that's my daughter. She bolted when my wife looked away."

"Gloria?"

"Yes, Gloria," Roger said, looking back at Hal, his eyes narrowed.

"She's a wonderful woman. I'm glad you could have children. I know she always wanted them," Hal said, swallowing hard. *And if she's the mother, I wonder who the real father is!*

Roger quickly moved to Hal's side. "She's adopted and if you tell a soul, I'll hunt you down and castrate you," he whispered harshly.

"I see the family resemblance," Hal said, non-plussed by the threat. "That's my Grace up there with her now." He patted Roger on the shoulder. "Your secret never left my lips," he whispered, "and never will. No hard feelings, I hope."

Roger's shoulders slumped in embarrassment. "I'm sorry. Really, I am, Hal. I heard through the rumor mill that *she* is gone. I never should have let her get between us."

"Divorced and it didn't cost me a dime," Hal said softly. "Other than a one-way ticket to Costa Rica. Congratulations on having a daughter. They're the greatest joy but can give you the greatest scares, too. I lost Grace for a while there, but she's back. That's her husband coming over to watch them now. Come on. Let me introduce you."

"Daddy!" Vickie squealed, lunging for her father, ignoring the gap between him and her pink pony.

Grace caught her and held her tight, memorizing the feel of the soft yet sturdy body in her arms, the scent of shampoo and excitement, the sound of her squeals at being reunited with a parent. A sound she'd never hear from the children she'd lost.

The group walked away from the carousel, Vickie now clutching her daddy close. "Join us for a drink?" Hal asked. "We have plenty."

"I'll go get some little cups," Dusty offered, then went back to the concession stand.

"Don't ever do that again," Roger scolded Vickie, his face furrowed with concern, a tear escaping from the corner of his eye at the thought of losing his treasure. "You scared your mother and me... Oh, shoot. Stay here with Uncle Hal and Cousin Gracie. I have to call Mommy and let her know I found you."

Grace held onto the four-year-old as they watched Dusty pour the thick peach-colored confection into the cup. "Be careful," she warned. "It's messy. And don't drink it too fast."

"Brain freeze!" Vickie said, then giggled. "That really hurts, huh?"

Hal sat back and watched the pair interact, fantasizing of how it would be when Grace and Dusty had their own child. Or would have been if Grace's twins had survived...

He shook his head. No bad thoughts today. Reunited with an estranged cousin: one huge blessing. Grace and Dusty discovering a new relative, another big blessing. Maybe this encounter would kick Grace's hormones into gear, or realign whatever was keeping her from getting pregnant. Dusty had already been tested and verified as potent. The results from her visit with the fertility specialist this morning would be back in less than two weeks. Now all they could do was wait. And pray.

Roger handed Hal his business card that he had added his home and cellphone numbers to. "Call me anytime. We can get together. At least, if it isn't too uncomfortable with you and Gloria."

"Um," Hal stalled, trying not to think of the woman he had wanted to marry but instead thinking of the opportunity for Grace to have 'good' family to get to know. "I think it would be fine. I know Grace has had some trouble conceiving. Maybe she and Gloria can share a few secrets. Or not. I'll leave it up to you." Hal pulled a card out of his wallet, scribbled his personal contact info on the back, and handed it to Roger. "We're still just outside of Plymouth. I let the kids have my place. I'm up the road at the bachelor's pad. You remember Doc Armstrong and Silas, right?"

Roger paled, then nodded. "Doc had three sons, didn't he? And didn't they start calling him Papa Doc after one of them became a doctor, too?"

"Yup. But a heads up if you come out to see us. He's kinda, sorta out of sons. The first one was murdered by the second one – who's in prison doing life – and the third one has been missing for four years. A little family drama there; not worth going into. I'm sure Chuck will come around again one of these days."

"Yeah, family is family. When you least expect it, we're there for each other. How many years has it been for us?" Roger asked.

"Way too many," Hal said. "Tell Gloria I said hi, and congratulations to both of you for having one of the most beautiful daughters in the world. I'm a little prejudiced there, though. I don't think you saw Grace when she was that age, but your little Vickie could be her clone. They're identical all the way down to those little ears that stick out just enough to be precious. Little angel ears, I call them."

"Must come down the mother's line, then," Roger said with a wink. *Keep the adoption part a secret, Cousin. We can still claim these two girls are related without referring to Victoria the Viper-mother and aunt.*

Chapter 2: Bad News & a Birthday

Two weeks later

"Did we have to come into the city for this?" Dusty asked. "I mean, couldn't the doctor just tell us what was wrong over the phone or call in a prescription or something?"

"I know they usually want to have a little visual going on at the same time. Posters and plastic models and such," Grace said, then brought up her finger, ready to chew on her cuticle again.

Dusty caught her eye, then grinned. "Tabasco," he whispered.

"Don't you dare!" she hissed, then giggled. "Just the thought of it keeps me from doing it. But you're right. I need a little reminder every once in a while. Nervous energy is not good. I think I'll bring my crocheting with me next time. I can't keep my hands still."

"We have so many afghans now, I think we're going to have to start giving them away."

"I already did," Grace said. "You only see the ones I make in the evening when you're home. I make at least three shawls a week and take them right to the hospital for newborns and mommies."

"Shawls for babies?" Dusty asked.

"Shawls for the mommies to use while they're nursing the babies…" Grace sighed in longing and frustration, then huffed. "What's taking them so long?"

"It's a doctor's office. That's what they do."

Grace looked around and saw that she wasn't the only one with the anxious pallor and tight lips. She tried to smile at another woman whose eye she had caught, then realized they were both grimacing at what was sure to be bad news for both of them. She shrugged her shoulder and looked down at her hands, then twiddled her thumbs. Another clinic. Another doctor.

Dusty set his hand on top of hers. "Just a few more minutes, and then we'll know. I'm sure it's good news or they wouldn't make us wait so long," he said, hoping his wishful speculation was more fact than fantasy.

"Mr. and Mrs. Rhodes?" the nurse called out, scanning the room. "Come on back."

Grace got to her feet, then faltered, nerves taking away her ability to lock her knees. "I got you," Dusty whispered, his arm around her waist.

"That's the only thing that keeps me going," Grace whispered back.

The nurse ushered the couple into the doctor's office, totally bypassing the exam rooms. "Uh, oh," Dusty whispered. "I don't know if this is good or bad."

"Bad," Grace said, covering her mouth to keep from losing the light breakfast she'd eaten.

Dusty leaned forward and looked for a trash can, but was stilled by Grace's hand. "I got it," she said, then sat back, composed. "It is what it is."

The bald and rotund doctor came in and greeted the young couple. "Let me be blunt," he said. "I see from your records that you were delivered of twins approximately four years ago via cesarean section. There were no hospital records that we could find..." he said, waiting for Grace to complete his thought.

"It was a private clinic," she said. "The doctor told me the twins died. That's why I know I'm not barren. I've conceived before."

"Uh, huh..."

"And my husband was tested three years ago. He's got very active sperm. They even wanted him as a donor!" Grace tried to contain her anger and frustration but it spilled out. "So, if I can conceive twins and carry them to over eight months gestation," she said vehemently, "and my husband has swimmers that are so active that the fertility folks wanted his boys for building tall blond babies, why can't we have a baby together? I mean, we did it before!"

"Because, my dear," the doctor said with as much compassion as he could, "the doctor or nurse or whoever delivered you, tied your tubes when he was in there. You had a tubal ligation. You have

12

healthy eggs but no way for them to get to the uterus."

"I'll kill him," Grace hissed. "If I ever see that Dr. Buddy again, I swear to God and to anything holy or unholy, I'll kill him!"

"Oh…Dr. Buddy…" the doctor said.

"You know him?" Grace asked, turning back to Dusty. He shrugged his shoulders, clueless.

"He was arrested about three, maybe four, years ago. He had a series of birthing clinics all up and down the east coast. He'd bring in pregnant women who wanted to give their babies up for adoption, give them a wonderful place to stay while gestating, then deliver them."

"Yeah. That's pretty much what happened to me. So, that's illegal?" Grace asked.

"What came next was. He'd deliver healthy babies, sell them – which is illegal – to desperate families, then tell the new parents the baby had died. Of course, that meant that he had a child he could resell many times over."

"The scum!" Dusty hissed.

"Ah," the doctor continued, "but it didn't stop there. He sedated the mothers so they didn't know their babies were still alive. While he was in them, he sterilized them, just as he did with you."

"But why?" Grace asked.

"Not only sterilized them but kept them as breeding stock. This way, he could promote a healthy vessel to prospective parents looking for surrogates. No chance of the mother having a child from her own eggs. He was a white slaver. You're lucky to be free. Many young women who went to his clinics to deliver children for adoption are still missing."

"Yeah, well, there was some intervention there. My friend got in the middle of that," Grace said, then looked at Dusty and grimaced.

"Was he an accomplice?" the doctor asked, leaning forward in his seat, eager to hear her answer. "Because if he was, he might have information that will help the authorities find these missing women."

"No, he didn't aid and abet or anything like that, I'm sure. I don't know where he is, though. I do know he's the reason I'm free. From what my father told me, they were setting me up in a recovery house but told him I was going to be somewhere else. He found out where I was and sent my dad and Dusty to come and get me. So, back to my fertility…"

"Yes…"

"Does that mean that I can be my own surrogate or whatever you call it?"

"Yes, we can fertilize the eggs outside of your body and implant them. It's called *in vitro fertilization*. We've been doing it since the late 70s. It's pricey but relatively safe. It doesn't work every time, but we can use your own eggs and his sperm. Does this sound like something you'd like to pursue?"

A sudden chill went up Grace's arms. She looked at Dusty and saw that he looked like he was the one ready to vomit this time. "Not right now," she said. "We'll get back to you."

Grace stood up and reached for Dusty's hand. "Come on. I want to go home." She looked at the doctor and blinked twice. A glimmer of familiarity sparked between them and then was gone. "Thanks for your time."

She reached out for her queasy husband. "Come on," she said and led him out of the office.

Once in the hallway, a dazed Dusty made his way to the fountain. "Just a sec. I'm thirsty."

"Sure. Why don't you go in the john and splash some water on your face, too. That might help."

Grace paced while she waited outside the men's bathroom. Nerves on edge, her hand flew towards her mouth. "Ah, to hell with it," she grumbled, then chewed at her cuticle. "Damn baby thieves!"

"What's wrong?" Dusty asked, seeing that she was back to her bad habit but positive that now was not the time to say, 'Tabasco.'

"I think this doctor was in cahoots with Dr. Buddy. Did you see the way he was positively radiant when he said Buddy had been busted? He wants to find those baby-making mamas for himself! He's got dozens, scores of couples looking for a ripe place to plant seeded eggs. I wouldn't trust him to put my egg with your sperm back into my body, even if I watched the procedure from start to finish. Damn! Damn! Damn!"

"Grace, you're going to have to trust someone, sometime," Dusty said, his hand on her shoulder.

"Yeah, well, I trust you, my dad, Silas, and Papa Doc. Even if he's been gone for four years, I'd trust Chuck, too. I know Papa Doc thinks he's still alive, but I can't believe he wouldn't at least check in on me."

"Um, Gracie, I think we need to talk," Dusty said. "But not here. Let's take a walk. You got me paranoid about security cameras now."

"I do? When did I ever talk about security cameras?"

"Walk," Dusty said. He put his arm around her shoulder, not willing to accept any discussion on the subject. "Outside, fresh air." *Traffic noises, people walking past us…*

"Can we even get to the parking garage this way?" Grace asked.

"Yup," Dusty said, pushing the door open for her.

"Why are you being so weird?"

Dusty put his hand on her shoulder and led her toward the little city park across the street. "Wait to talk."

He spotted an empty picnic table and used a found newspaper to sweep off the bench seat. "Did you realize that after what he just said, our babies may still be alive?"

"Wait! What? Oh, my God! No! I mean, yes! They could still be alive?"

"Sounds reasonable to me. I know you got the chills talking to him. Did you recognize him or something?"

"Yes. I was sedated a lot of the time. Come to think of it, I remember going under and the anesthesiologist made a crack about Chuck's upset stomach being morning sickness. Shit! He knows who I am!"

"Well, for right now, I'm going to agree with you about no invasive procedures to make a baby. Let's give it a year or so and see if we can find our children," Dusty said.

"I don't know if it's delayed maternal hormones or not, but I'm on a roll now!" Grace said.

Yeah, and now I don't feel obligated to tell you that Chuck really is alive and well. That secret can come out later. I just hope I don't trip myself up! The guys would kill me if I spilled the beans!

***

January 2, 1996

"Hal? Yeah, this is Roger. Hey, I hate to do this to you at the last minute like this, but we're having a birthday party for Vickie Lynn tomorrow and wanted to know if you and your beautiful daughter and her husband wanted to come by and say hi. Yeah, well, I would have said something when I saw you, but Gloria was organizing it, and I didn't want to step on her toes. Neither one of us thought about you until Vickie Lynn asked if we were going to go see that 'ooni-corn' lady again. Yeah, Grace really made an impression on her. Well, we're still at the same place. Light snacks around four-ish if you don't have to work too late. I thought you and those old guys might want to pop in and sing happy birthday to my little miracle baby, too. There won't be that many kiddos around but there'll be plenty of *hors d'oeuvres*, cake, and sangria for everyone. Bring the gang. No, don't worry about upsetting anyone or stirring up hard feelings. I think Gloria wants to see if you're still the hunk you were in college. Yeah, well, put a hat on so that shiny bald spot doesn't blind her. Hey! Someone in the family had to keep all his hair! All right. See at least three of you tomorrow, then."

***

Knock! Knock!

"Hey, Dad. What's going on?" Dusty asked Hal. "You look like you just sold your portfolio at twice its estimated value."

"Nah, I'm not even thinking about work until half-way into

16

January. This being semi-retired at forty-five is great! Hey, how's Gracie doing?"

"She's still bummed that she was sterilized, but she does have a fire under her that keeps her getting up in the morning. She's up at daylight or earlier, searching the internet for news stories about *in vitro fertilization* procedures in other countries. At least it's keeping her from depression. I'd rather see her fuming than a lump under the covers."

"Yeah," Hal agreed. "You and me and everyone else. Three years was enough! So, the reason I'm so perky is that we've been invited to a birthday party. Remember Grace's little cousin we met at the carousel a couple of weeks ago?"

"Your cousin's daughter?"

"Yup. She's four-years-old tomorrow. Roger and his wife invited us over for her birthday party."

"Um, Dad… You do know what tomorrow is, don't you?"

"The day after today?" Hal quipped, then looked down at his watch to verify the date. "Oh, crap."

"Yup, it's the day she lost the babies. Oh, and before you tell her what's going on, can I tell you something?"

"Of course." Hal pulled out a kitchen chair and sat down. "Do you need anything? Are the guys downtown giving you fits?"

"No, they're cool. They got over me being a blue-collar guy right after I pointed out the holes in their proposals. Now they call me The Natural."

"Good for you. Now, what's on your mind?"

"We told you about the doctor's visit. Sort of. What Grace didn't tell you was that the specialist she saw was the anesthetist who was there when she had the babies. He was sort of fishing for where Chuck was. You see…Well, this is a biggie. This guy said that this Dr. Buddy who delivered Grace would tell the adopting parents that the babies had died. This way, he got to keep all their money, and still had babies to sell to other parents."

"Oh, shit!" Hal slumped sideways in his chair, nearly fainting while seated. "And you think that maybe her twins didn't die? That they're out there somewhere?"

"That's the first thing I thought of, too. It didn't hit her right away, though. She'd already been dealing with so much guilt about doing something wrong while pregnant and that's why they died, that she couldn't see the proverbial forest for the trees when he mentioned it. So, somewhere out there, there might be a couple of her children."

"And we don't even know if they're boys or girls or one of each…" Hal said.

"I was, and still am, going to let her tell you my suspicions in her own time. She didn't ask me *not* to tell you, so I'm not betraying a confidence. Still, I'd appreciate it if you didn't let on we already had this conversation."

"So, she's really searching the internet for clues about her babies?"

"Not the babies, per se, but Dr. Buddy and his cohorts. It seems they had – or still have – a series of homes where they keep women to carry surrogate babies."

"White slavery still exists," Hal said softly. "Damn!"

"Hey! What are you doing here, Dad?" Grace asked.

Startled, Hal sat up and took a deep breath to compose himself, then grinned, remembering the original purpose of his visit. "Just talking with The Natural here. We're invited to a birthday party tomorrow. Your little second cousin is having a birthday party, and we're invited."

"Vickie Lynn? Oh, that's right! She's so cute. She's at that age where when you ask her name, she gives you her age. Ask her age, and she gives you her name. Is she going to be four or five? She showed me four fingers, but I don't know if they taught her how old she was or would be."

Hal shook his head and said, "I guess we'll find out tomorrow when we count the candles, won't we? Anyone for a shopping trip into the city to find her a gift?"

"We don't need to," Grace said. "I already have the perfect one. I have a stuffed pink unicorn that she's going to love. I'll just clean it up and add a big ribbon, and she's good to go. As a matter of fact…"

Hal and Dusty watched as Grace's face twitched in recall. "Yes…" Hal prompted.

"I got that doll for my fifth birthday! I've had it for nearly twenty years. Pinkie's ready for a new home. She looks great on the shelf, but really needs someone to play with."

Dusty and Hal both noticed her tears escaping but didn't comment. They both knew Grace had been saving that magical stuffed animal for her own child. Giving it away – whether to a relative or not – meant that she was finally moving on.

"You're right," Hal said, standing up to hug her. "The perfect gift."

***

"Here goes nothing," Hal mumbled so only Papa Doc could hear.

Or so he thought.

"If only we could be that lucky," Silas said softly. "I remember the last time I was here…"

The door opened swiftly at the soft tap of the brass knocker, as if someone was standing behind it, waiting. "Hey, there!" Roger said, hand out ready to greet whoever he saw first with a hearty handshake.

"Long time, no see," Papa Doc said, then moved away so Silas could have his own moment of personal discomfort.

"Sounds like congratulations are about four – or is it five? – years too late," Silas said, returning the firm grip with a minimal pump of the traditional handshake.

"Four. Vickie Lynn is four-years-old today. It doesn't seem like it, though. Sometimes it seems like it was only yesterday she came into our lives. The next minute, it's like she's always been a part of our family. I can't imagine what it's going to be like when she

19

grows up and moves away."

"Do your best not to think about it," Hal said, then stepped back.

"Enjoy them every minute," Papa Doc added, his eyes misting. "One minute, they're under your feet and you can't wait for them to take off to school, the next, you're wondering where they are."

"Or worse," Silas whispered, then grimaced, thinking of Papa Doc's first son dead, killed by the second one who was in prison, the third one – Chuck – lying low and living off the grid somewhere in the backwoods of America.

Roger saw the familial interaction, like a visible electric current, a common thought moving from one man to the other. All four of them had been acquainted for more than twenty years, but those three now seemed more like the cousins he and Hal used to be. One man's reflections were shared by the other two. Like an old married couple, these three were in sync, comfortable in their lives.

"I brought something for Vickie Lynn," Grace said, holding up a bright bag stuffed with pink tissue paper. "It used to be mine but I'm sure she'll love it."

"She'll love it even more, then," Roger said, ushering her in. "A family heirloom."

"Hello there, Dusty, is it?" he asked, letting the last of the family group in.

"Yes, sir," Dusty said, then craned his neck to catch sight of the little birthday girl. "We love children and hope to have some of our own soon."

"Well, I hope you don't have to wait as long as Gloria and I did. Over fifteen years of trying and then, boom! A baby. Of course," he whispered loud enough so the men could hear, "the trying was fun."

Dusty felt his face redden, so held one finger up in agreement, covering most of his glow with the gesture.

"Oh, my!" Grace said, looking around the room. Dozens of unicorns filled the area, from piñatas to posters to the ice sculpture in the middle of a fountain of pink punch.

"Well, I *may* have gone a little overboard," Gloria said, coming up to greet Grace.

"Yeah, well, they're only young once. She may not appreciate this much attention when she's a teenager, but for now, enjoy it."

"Oh, I do enjoy it! I feel as if I'm in my second childhood. Oh, and you probably don't remember me. I'm your Aunt Gloria, but please, just call me Gloria. No one needs to know we're related *that way.*"

Grace chuckled, glad that Gloria didn't want to bring up that her sister, Victoria, was her mother. "Yes, my father's cousin's wife is close enough to being my aunt, but Gloria works for me, too. Where's our birthday girl?"

"Oh, she's upstairs. I just got a nanny for her. Not that she really needs a nanny. Roger and I did everything for her since the day she was born. Elsa is more of her tutor. Most parents send their children away to preschool at four, but I'm not ready to part with her. Besides," she whispered, "you never know what the children they're associating with will be like. It's not really the kids so much…" She shook her head and pursed her lips. "But some children's parents…"

"Tell me about it. Or rather, let's not. Where should I put this?"

Gloria took the bag Grace offered and set it on the table laden with exotically-wrapped gifts, a miniature battery-powered Rolls Royce with a huge pink ribbon parked beneath it.

"I'd say it sucks having a birthday so close to Christmas," Grace said, "but it looks like she still managed to do well."

Roger came over and put his hand on Grace's shoulder. "I think my wife gives her too much in the way of material goods, but we tell Vickie Lynn that she has to take care of what she has or we'll give it away to someone who will appreciate it. So far, so good."

"And here she comes now," Gloria said, her smile bright at watching the young girl come down the steps one-by-one, poised as a real princess, her hand gently waving to the fifteen or so adults and half dozen children at the bottom of the stairs.

"Wow! What an entrance! And where did you get that dress?" Grace asked.

"One of my friends is a close friend of Christian Dior. He designed it for her. It's my gift to her."

"Oh, my. You might want to get her a life-sized doll made so when she grows out of it, the dress won't go to waste."

"Already commissioned," Gloria said. "She's getting a real twin…"

Gloria started coughing as soon as the word was out of her mouth, gagging on the memory that somewhere in the backwoods of Oregon and California, her daughter really did have a twin. Or rather, two.

Grace wrapped her arm around Gloria's waist, ready to help her to a chair when she was waved off. "No, I'm fine. I just swallowed wrong," she whispered hoarsely then looked up to watch her daughter continue her entrance.

Vickie Lynn was still taking her time descending the staircase, heeding the prompts from the nanny three feet behind her. "Smile, little one. Show those perfect teeth."

However, when the miniature beauty queen spotted Grace, all poise and charm blew up into unbridled excitement and passion, arms waving and voice squealing. "Ooni-corn Lady! You came!"

Rushing down the last four steps, Vickie Lynn tumbled forward, her foot catching on the leading edge of the gown of pink chiffon, seed pearls, and lace. Six adults rushed to catch her, but it was Grace who wound up with her in her arms. "Are you all right?"

"You came!" Vickie Lynn said, swiping the curled ringlets out of her face with a sputter. "I asked Daddy for you for my present and he said you'd come. Maybe. But if you came, I couldn't keep you. Are you sure you don't want to live with me, Ooni-corn Lady? We can go ride the carousel all day long. That is if you drive us there. I got a car from my Aunt, but I can't go past the front yard, Mommy said."

Grace brushed the curls behind Vickie's ears, noticing they

22

stuck out just like hers. "I can't stay here all the time, but I can come and see you whenever your mommy and daddy say I can. I do have to work sometimes, though."

"Is she okay?" Roger asked, his bottom lip sucked in with fear.

"She just messed up her hair a bit. You should be an acrobat. You landed on your feet pretty fast," Grace said. "Here, honey. Give your daddy a big hug and a squeeze. You scared him."

Roger picked her up and held her close, pivoting so he could see Gloria. His head shook minimally, a silent admonishment that her overzealousness for a show had almost injured their daughter.

'I'm sorry,' Gloria mouthed, her watery eyes proving her sincerity.

"Thank you for bringing Ooni-corn Lady, Daddy," Vickie said, reaching out to touch her.

"My name is Grace," she said. "Do you know what my name means?"

"Ooni-corn Lady!" Vickie Lynn declared.

"Yeah, I think it does," Roger said, then winked at Grace. "Thanks for coming. Double thanks since that's twice you've saved her from falling on her face."

"I'll be there for her anytime you need me," Grace said. "And I babysit for free," and added a wink.

"I'm not a baby," Vickie said.

"Okay. I 'pretty little girl' sit for free," Grace said.

Everyone within earshot laughed, then started milling around. Excitement for Act One was over. Excitement for Act Two – the opening of presents and eating of cake – was coming soon.

***

Eight years later

Elsa looked at the slip of paper with the phone number. She hated to bring anyone else into her world of extortion but after eight years, her garden of blackmail sources was depleted. She needed more information. Or proof for some of her suspicions. After all these years of operating solo, she didn't want to admit she needed anyone, especially a man. She snorted in frustration and dialed.

"Hello, Jimmy? Yes, you don't know me, but you come highly recommended. No, I'm not the police or a lawyer. I want photos if you can get them, but I also hear you have a directional microphone. There's a certain young woman I want you to follow. No, not all the time. I'll give you a heads up when she's with the Thornwhistle's daughter. Oh, so you do know that family. Yes, their only child is twelve-and-a-half years old. I suspect that a certain Grace Rhodes is her biological mother. Yes, I want you to listen in on the pair's conversations. Do you think you can do that? Well, I don't give a flying fart about anyone else. I pay well. You won't have to trail behind pop stars and aging country singers anymore. I have your number. I'll give you a call the next time they're together. No. You don't need to know my name. Just call this number with any information."

Click.

"That should restart the revenue stream," Elsa said with a sneer of perverted pleasure. "Try and get rid of me when she starts high school, will you, Roger Thornwhistle! I've just begun to harvest your wealth!"

Chapter 3: Growing Up is Hard to Do

January 3, 2005

"Are you sure she wants us at her birthday party?" Dusty asked. He helped himself to a cup of coffee and croissant from the buffet the Thornwhistles always had set up for visitors. He pulled up a chair and sat next to Grace. "I mean, she's thirteen years old now. She's sure to want just friends her own age. Old folks hanging around are just boring."

"No, we're worse, even if we aren't that old. We're embarrassing. That's my job: to make her blush in front of her friends."

"Grace!" Dusty yelped.

"No, I'm messing with you. I remember how giddy and ridiculous I was at that age. I knew everything." Grace blanched and shook her head, trying to forget the sneers and mean words her mother tormented her with when she was growing up.

"Are you all right?" Dusty asked. "You look all pasty – like you had another one of those flashbacks."

"Yeah, I did. In my mother's opinion, everything I did, said, or wore was stupid or ugly." She snorted in derision. "I never would have made it this far if it hadn't been for my father and Sally, the housekeeper. Dad would literally tell me *not* to listen to anything she said. Well, except they did agree on one thing…"

"What's that?"

"They both said don't have sex until I was married. And not to get married until after I had finished college." Grace rolled her eyes. "I guess that's two things. Oh, well. So much for going to college. Now with the internet, I can do all the studying and research I want online."

"I was glad I could skip right to starting a business. All I needed was a little direction from your dad and a foot in the door with the right advertising firms and bankers. Rhodes and Gardens made it onto the Fortune 500 this month, too! Who thought creating a franchise for groundskeeping and snowplowing would work? Hey, is it true that your Dad and the guys are going to Nepal this year?"

"Nope."

"What do you mean, nope?"

"They just started that rumor to flush out some of the *paparazzi* who have started nosing around again."

"Who are they following and why?" Dusty asked, picking up the croissant to dunk in his coffee.

"Me," Grace said. "And before you ask again, I don't know why."

"Maybe it's because you spend a lot of time with Vickie Lynn and you two just happen to look a lot like…" Dusty suggested, his eyes squinted in anticipation of another argument.

"Like mother and daughter? Hey, as long as Gloria's busy with her charities and Roger says it's all right, I want to spend as much time I can with her during her formative years. That snide bitch of a nanny they insist on keeping around keeps poisoning Vickie's outlook on just about everything. Did you know I heard her actually lecture Vickie on how poor people are dumb? That if they were smart, they'd have money?"

"What?"

Grace nodded her head, eyebrows furrowed as if she was boring a hole through Nanny Elsa's forehead. "I can't explain it, but I have an intense hatred for that woman."

"Well, poisoning our daughter's outlook on life is a biggie. Maybe I can have a word with Roger…"

"Don't. We agreed a long time ago to stay in the background in Vickie's life. There's no way I could tear her away from them. I know you can't measure love, but if you could, I'd say it was an absolute four-way tie on which one of us loved Vickie the most. Besides, there's no way I want to alienate anyone and not even be a spectator to what's going on in her life."

"So, do you think that one of the *paparazzi* suspects you're the biological mother?"

"That's what the Dads think. Silas said he was sure that the fat bald guy is Jimmy grown old ungracefully. Remember I told you that my mother knew I was pregnant, that she saw me just before Chuck got me to Dr. Buddy's home clinic?"

"Yeah, and then she shot you!" Dusty said, his fists balled up on either side of his coffee cup.

"All she'd have to do is tell Jimmy to follow me and eavesdrop with one of those fancy mics; listen for me to say something revealing to Vickie. Of course, I never would, so there's no story there. Those guys are a nuisance, but there's nothing to record or sell to the tabloids. If there *was* something that proved we were Vickie Lynn's parents, one of us would have found it years ago."

"And what would we have done with it if we had found it?" Dusty asked, wiping the crumbs off his fingers.

"Even if I found it today, I'd still do absolutely nothing. I have to wonder if Gloria and Roger know who adopted the other twin, though. Something tells me they do."

"I agree there. That lifesize twin doll she keeps in her office, dressed in the Dior Vickie wore on her fourth birthday, is kind of spooky."

"No, what's spooky is the way she glances back and forth between it and Vickie when she's in the room. I was only there once when it happened. Gloria noticed me watching her. I must have looked stunned or shocked or something because she remarked about it. "Just like she had a twin, huh?"

"I was there, remember?" Dusty said. He pushed his coffee cup away, uncomfortable at recalling their loss. "There's no doubt in my mind that she knows there's a twin. We just have to make sure she doesn't know that we know. I don't want to lose our unofficial godparents status."

"Amen to that," Grace said. "But that doesn't mean I'm going to stop looking."

"Back at ya on that amen."

"Do I look pretty?" Vickie asked, startling them as she came into the room unannounced. She turned around slowly to present her lace over satin pale blue gown, the tight bodice and pushup bra creating a body beyond her thirteen years of age. Earrings dripping with jewels and a matching diamond and sapphire necklace pointed to the spot where cleavage would be in a few years. A simple diamond tiara was nestled in the coif of curls piled on top of her head, a reluctant smile on her face.

"Pretty is too tame a word," Grace said. "You're stunning!"

"Uh, huh!" Dusty proclaimed. "But you're only thirteen. I mean, you look much older. Or, rather, you're dressed like it."

Vickie came over to the table with them and plopped down, very unladylike. "I hate it. I know I should be grateful, but diamonds aren't for everyone. I'd rather have ripped denim jeans, a tank top, and a flannel shirt. I know I could order them – and I have in the past – but as soon as Nanny Elsa finds them, they're in the trash. Or even worse – she burns them in the incinerator! Then I have to listen to her lecture for a week about how we need to show our best side to everyone all the time, how rich people are better and need to remind the lower class."

"You don't believe her, do you?" Grace asked.

"No. I rarely believe anything she says. If it's not in one of my school books, I just take it as her opinion, not fact."

"Opinions are like belly buttons," Grace said. "Everyone has one."

Vickie started to giggle. "That's almost the same thing Daddy says only he uses another part of the human anatomy."

"Yeah, well, I didn't want to say asshole," Grace said, then giggled, too.

"Tell you what," Dusty said, acknowledging the old joke with a grin and a head shake of 'enough, already,' now wanting to change the subject. "You go ahead and let Grace know what you want for clothes. We'll order them and you can wear them when you hang out with us. Maybe we can talk your parents into letting you come camping with us for the weekend. Would you like to learn how to fish?"

"Really? I mean, yeah! That would be the best birthday present ever! Just don't let Nanny Elsa know. She's sure to find a way to ruin it for us."

"Our secret," Dusty said.

"Ours and your parents," Grace added. "I'm sure they agree that Nanny Elsa doesn't have to rule your whole life."

"I can't wait to go to high school, just so she's out of my life." Vickie reached up and took out her earrings. "And these things are so heavy! I want to wear little gold hoops like you, Grace."

"We'll get you some of those to wear when you're camping, too," Dusty said. "Country chic."

"Now I'll look just like you, Grace!" Vickie said more brightly than usual. *Just like the mom who gave birth to me!*

Grace looked at Dusty looked and shrugged, the mischievous twinkle in Vickie's eye not missed by either of the 'godparents.' *She suspects! Don't you say a word, and I won't either.*

***

January 3, 2008
Three years later

"Can you believe our little girl is going to be sixteen?" Roger asked Gloria.

His wife leaned closer to the mirror, then pulled back, scowling. "As of today, she *is* sixteen. Hmm. It used to be that the closer I got to the mirror, the better I could see. Now I have to move back. And reading is even more difficult. My arms are almost too short to read the newspaper now."

"Well," Roger said, chuckling, "There's nothing but crap and gossip in that society section you're so fond of. And if you can't get far enough away from the mirror to inspect for new wrinkles, that's a good thing."

"What? Why?"

"Which one? Both. It's good you can't read that garbage *and* that your brain isn't being poisoned by someone else's opinion of our friends and business associates. Plus, it's great that you're not stressing about itty bitty laugh lines." Roger leaned over his wife and gave her a kiss on top of the head. "You always have been and always will be the most beautiful woman in the world."

"What about Vickie Lynn?" Gloria asked.

"You, my dear, have the benefit of your beauty being enhanced by my true love for and devotion to you. Our daughter has raw beauty and innocence. She's simply the most beautiful *young* woman in the world."

Gloria snorted in frustration. "She and her two sisters. I really do wish Chuck and Leanne and Luther would reach out again. It's been how many years since Leanne and Luther sent a family picture?"

"That was only two years ago," Roger said.

"Well, that one didn't count. Tori Lynn was wearing a ski mask. We couldn't see what she looked like. Plus she was wearing a snowsuit. Who knows if she's fat or skinny or…"

"Slow down, Gloria," Roger said, standing behind her to look in the mirror. "I think your hormones are getting in the way of common sense again. Luther and Leanne are great parents. For God's sake, they're botanists! They're feeding her the best natural foods on the planet. That girl has probably never even had a bite of junk food in her life! They're all happy. Let them bring her up their way."

"Yes, but we've never even seen Chuck's little girl. Not even a fuzzy snapshot."

"So, when was the last time you heard from him?" Roger asked, adjusting his tie.

"Probably two years ago. He sent a money order from West Virginia. He did include a little note, telling me thanks for the loan – we should be caught up now."

"I wish he hadn't done that," Roger said. "I was more than happy to help him out until he could get his mobile clinic established. You did burn it, didn't you?"

"The clinic?" Gloria asked.

"The money order."

"You asked me to, didn't you?" Gloria replied, not wanting to let him know she had kept it as a memento – her one link to their daughter's other triplet sister.

Roger nodded and sighed. He wouldn't push her. She had saved it. Just like every other photo or scrap of contact pertaining to the other two girls. Whether she was being obsessive, compulsive, or just a little bit nuts, it was who she was – his Gloria.

***

"Nanny Elsa, how do I look?" Vickie asked.

"A little chubby, but not too bad," the stern taskmaster said, pushing the girl's waistline in with her bony index finger.

"If I eat any less, I'll lose all my boobs! As it is, I'm only eating eight hundred calories a day. And not even one carb! If I ever smell tuna again, I think I'm going to puke!"

"Puking's good," Elsa said. "You can enjoy the food, then purge it without adding a calorie. Just make sure you rinse your mouth afterward or it will eat the enamel from your teeth."

"But my boobs!"

"You can buy boobs. Just ask your father for a nice set of double-D's as another birthday present. I'm sure he'll say yes. All men like big boobs."

"I don't know about that…" Vickie said, looking in the mirror at her reshaped ears. "He and Mama both threw a fit when I asked to have my ears fixed. I know you said they looked horrid the way they stuck out, but Mom and Dad always said they were so cute. Angel ears they called them. Are you sure they won't throw a fit when they find out you took me to the doctor and had them clipped?"

"Your mother and I have an agreement. She won't discharge me," Elsa said, her smirk of control uninhibited.

"She must really like you. Most of my friends lost their live-in nannies and tutors by middle school. It seems your only duty these days is that of personal dresser and confidant."

"It keeps me busy," Elsa said. *And rich!*

Vickie twisted her curly locks together and set the bundle on top of her head, then let it go. "Do you think I should wear my hair up or down?"

"Ah, wear it up to show off those new ears that lay so flat to the side of your head."

"But won't my parents notice?"

Elsa shrugged, her smirk of domination returning. "What are they going to do about it? The deed has been done. It's your body, isn't it?"

Vickie slumped on the stool, depressed that she had let anyone talk her into changing her looks. She was insecure enough about her body image. All her life, her parents had told her how beautiful she was. Now every freckle and curve were under intense scrutiny and criticism from Nanny Elsa. Sometimes she felt as if she'd be better off without her. At least her self-esteem wouldn't be under constant attack. Still, she was only sixteen. Just two more years until she could make her own decisions. She was doing well on class credits. She'd graduate early – at the semester break – and hit the road as soon as she was eighteen. That would probably be the only way to get rid of that skinny Swedish gray-haired guilt dispenser!

"Here, let me arrange your hair. I'll loan you this antique comb for the evening. It's been in my family for generations. It should set off the tresses perfectly."

Vickie Lynn sat at her dressing table and watched as Elsa deftly arranged her curling iron-enhanced curls into a cascade atop her head, letting a few tresses drift down one side, then securing them with the gem-encrusted heirloom her father had told her would be hers one day. *Why did Nanny Elsa say it was hers? Now is not the time to challenge her ownership. Then again, it never is a good time to contest anything she says!*

Vickie picked up the mirror and turned around to look at the back of her coif. She glanced down and saw the incision the doctor had cut in the back of her ear. The cut itself was nearly invisible, but the area around it was red and swollen. Nanny had lied! She said there was no chance of infection. She resisted the urge to touch it and verify it was fevered. It was best to play ignorant than acknowledge both the inflammation and the fact she'd been lied to. Unless her iron-willed matron was out of the room, she was watching her. Shoot! Even then, she felt as if she was a test subject under observation. She probably had nanny cams stashed everywhere.

For years, she'd felt like a flesh and blood android: told how to stand, sit, eat and speak. Life had been a blast when she was younger: riding her battery-powered Rolls Royce all through the house and gardens, going to the carousel with Mom and Dad, Grace and Dusty. Their weekly get-togethers were the highlight of growing up. When had all the fun stopped?

She didn't know the day because she wasn't aware of calendars and dates back then, but she did remember when. It was the day her mother introduced her to her nanny. Nanny Elsa.

"We'd like to keep you at home as much as possible," Mom had said, "so rather than go to pre-school with all those children who have cold and flu germs, we've hired a special teacher for you. This is Nanny Elsa. She's going to be living with us, too."

Mom tried to look happy about it but even at that early age – four or five – Vickie could tell the smile was fake. Dad didn't even try to smile. He kept bringing up the newspaper, pretending to look at it or turn the pages, then shake it and set it down, frowning. Vickie thought it was because he wasn't happy to have someone taking his place. Now that she knew Nanny Elsa, though, she knew it wasn't the nanny part he objected to; it was the Elsa part.

Suddenly, Vickie felt ill. The infection might be a part of it. Nearly starving herself for the last three weeks – so she could shrink down to the twenty-two-inch waistline Nanny Elsa insisted was essential for a young woman of breeding like herself – could be another contributing factor. But what really soured her stomach was seeing how she and her parents had been manipulated by Nanny Elsa for years. She knew the why for her: because she was a child. She knew she had to listen or would have to pay the consequences. Mom and Dad never saw the bruises from being pinched because they no longer helped with bathing. The one time Mom had seen the bruise on her backside when changing into her bathing suit at the beach house, Nanny Elsa made up a lie, saying she had bumped into the dresser.

Vickie set down the mirror and saw she was practically under a microscope again. Elsa was staring at her, her wire-rimmed glasses slipping down her nose. The warden pushed them back up. "Is something amiss?" she asked caustically – as if she could smell rebellion in the works.

"My stomach feels queasy. I don't know if I want to go…"

Elsa took three determined steps up to Vickie and grasped her chin, bringing it up to face her. "This is your sixteenth birthday party. Some very important people will be here this evening. You *will* be in attendance. And you *will* be on your best behavior. And you *won't* eat more than a carrot stick or drink more than sparkling water. Do. You. Understand?"

Vickie's heart felt like it was coming up through her mouth. Beating so hard, it felt like it had pumped itself up to basketball size and was rising, threatening to choke off her breath. She managed a nod, then Nanny Elsa let go. "Put some concealer on that chin. There's a red spot right there," she said, thumping the spot she had just let go of.

"Yes, Nanny Elsa," Grace said. *Do all sixteen-year-old daughters of billionaires wish they were dead or is it only me?*

***

"Here she comes," Dusty said, saluting Vickie Lynn with a glass of champagne.

"Our little girl is almost all grown up," Grace whispered. "Isn't she beautiful?"

Dusty sighed. "I'm sorry, but when I see her, I can't help but wonder if her twin was a girl or a boy. Can you imagine two young women that beautiful existing in the same world?"

"If I could just ask Gloria about it, and then rewind time so she didn't remember me asking – or even knowing that I was aware Vickie had a twin – I would. The way she looks at the life-size doll, though, my bet is that it was another girl."

"So, do you ever regret not having the procedure?"

"You mean in vitro fertilization? No. I keep busy enough with the human trafficking research. At least I was able to get Dr. Fat Boy busted and his clinic shut down. He may have been unsure about who I was when we went there for the test results, but he won't ever forget me now."

Grace set her champagne flute down and picked up a sparkling water with a lime wedge. "Plus, I really do believe that one of these days, we'll find our other twin. In the meantime, being the favorite aunt-type godmother and second cousin is good enough for me."

Dusty hugged her. "Me, too."

"Good evening." Vickie didn't even try to make her fake smile look real for Grace and Dusty. Her left eye twitched as a tear tried to form. "Thank you for coming this evening," she added mechanically, then bit her bottom lip, impending tears choking back her ability to even try for a real conversation.

Grace looked around the room quickly and spotted the iron maiden in the corner, her eyes like binoculars fixed on Vickie. She suddenly reached out and grabbed for Vickie, clutching for her as if she felt faint and needed her help. "Ladies room," she gasped.

Vickie totally forgot her problems and held onto Grace, supporting her. "I have you," she said.

"Here, let me help," Dusty offered, then caught the quick scowl from his wife. "Well, if you're sure you have her," he added, stepping back.

"Lady stuff," Grace gasped.

Vickie Lynn led her to the bathroom off her father's downstairs office, bypassing the rooms set aside for the guests. "Are you all

35

right? Are you pregnant? You look a little weird. I mean…" she babbled, concerned for Grace.

Grace stood up straight and stared Vickie in the eye. "What's wrong," she asked, then walked around her slowly, inspecting her for damages. She came back to stand in front of Vickie and noticed the smudge. She wiped the excess foundation away with her thumb, verifying the signs of abuse.

"I don't think your mother or father ever has or ever will lay a hand on you. That leaves only one person. Did that bitch Elsa do that to you?"

Vickie's mouth twitched into a smile as she sniffed. "You called her a bitch," she said, then allowed a small chuckle to escape.

"Well… I guess that means she did. I guess if she asks if you told anyone, you can truthfully say you didn't. Just nod if yes."

Vickie nodded, then the tears started falling.

"I'd say don't cry or you'll spoil your makeup," Grace said. "But if it makes you feel better, cry away. This isn't how a sixteenth birthday party is supposed to be. It should be a celebration, not a cover-up for a tyrant. So, yes or no question: do you know what Elsa has over your parents?"

"Huh?"

"I'll take that as a no. Look, you're enough of an adult that I can tell you a few things, including that there has to be some reason why your parents keep Elsa employed. I've seen the way your father looks at her. He absolutely loathes her. Your mother doesn't feel too kindly towards her, either. I mean, as far as I can tell, she barely tolerates her. And I know they'd do anything for you, but I really don't think they're keeping Elsa here because *you* want her."

"Oh, Lord in Heaven, no!"

"Well, I'll see what I can find out later. I know I had the most horrid mother in the world. I wanted someone to rescue me from her. My dad did the best he could to insulate me from her…"

"But my mother isn't horrid," Vickie interrupted.

"I know, I know. She's sort of in the position my dad was. I don't know what hold Elsa has over them, but I'm sure it's something."

"Grace, I know it's supposed to be a secret, but I have to ask you…"

Grace's eyes widened and her skin flushed. *Dear Lord in Heaven, did she find out I am her mother?* "Sweetheart, you can ask me anything." *I might not be able to give you an answer but before I start saying too much, let me hear your question.*

"Is my mother your mother's sister? I mean, everyone knows that your dad and my dad are first-cousins, but are you and I related, too?"

A wave of relief washed over Grace, a veritable horde of tingle gremlins rushing over her skin. "Yes, we are very much related. We are blood kin. And yes, your mother and my mother are sisters." *And how I wish I could tell you I'm your birth mother and only your cousin by virtue of adoption.*

"Wouldn't that make us double cousins or something?"

"Um, I'm not sure how that goes. If our fathers were brothers, then we'd be double cousins. Let's just say we're closely related. But let's keep that between you and me. As I said, I am not fond of my mother. She and Elsa are – or were – very much alike."

"Is she still alive?"

"Don't know. Don't really care. My dad said the only good thing that ever came out of her was me."

Vickie laughed at the old joke, causing Grace to give in to the giggles, too. "Are you ready to go back to your birthday bash?"

"Bash? For my birthday, I wish someone would bash her!"

"Ach. Don't worry. The night is young and Dusty's drinking champagne. Anything's possible."

The two interlocked elbows and came out together, all smiles and relief.

"Here they come!" Dusty said, walking briskly over to the now dimpled duo. "Are you all right?" he whispered.

"She just had a little gas," Vickie said, laughing anew at the thought of Dusty punching Elsa.

"There's my little girl. I guess you're not so little anymore now, though, are you?" Roger said, walking over to give her a big hug. He looked down and saw the heirloom hair comb in Vickie's hair, the latest piece of jewelry Elsa had blackmailed Gloria into giving her. His face reddened. *One of these days. I swear, one of these days I'm going to strangle that Swedish bitch!*

"Are you all right, Dad?"

"Yeah, are you all right, Roger?" Hal seconded. "First my daughter scoots out of the room before I even get the chance to say hello, and then you're all puce-colored."

Roger took three deep breaths, willing his blood pressure and rage down to socially acceptable levels, then remembered how important this night was for Vickie: his daughter's sweet sixteen party. He'd suck down just about anything for her.

"Yes, I'm fine. I might have to start taking blood pressure medicine, though. I didn't realize that the ladies had invited so many people – so many young men. Good Lord, I think every man of means from the east coast and his son is here tonight. What was Gloria thinking?"

Gloria came up behind him, her lips drawn tight, and tugged his elbow to get his attention. "It wasn't me," she hissed. "*Someone* decided she needed to take over the guest list and arrangements."

Roger felt his face start to redden again and immediately began the yoga breathing technique his doctor had suggested.

"Are you having a fit or something?" Hal asked, stepping in front of his cousin to block him from the view of the guests.

"No, it's an alternative method for controlling high blood pressure and anger management. It was either this or a pocketful of pills with a long list of side effects."

Hal watched as Roger's eyes narrowed in sheer loathing. He quickly turned around and looked behind him to see the target of the hatred. Yup, just as he suspected. The nanny, Elsa. "Why don't you just up and fire her?" Hal whispered.

Roger took another deep breath then blew it out. "I would if I could, but I can't. It's complicated."

"Well, you know if there's anything I can do to help you out of your *predicament*, I'm here for you." Hal paused as he realized there was something he could do. "Give me all the information you have on her: name, birthdate, where she was born, former employers, everything. Silas can probably even find out what toilet paper brand she used when she was twenty!"

Roger snorted with laughter, softly at first, then at a roar.

"It wasn't that funny," Hal said softly, now embarrassed at Roger's exaggerated reaction.

"Thanks. I needed that. The visual image of her wiping her ass… Yup, just what I needed." Roger playfully punched him in the upper arm, then moved around him. "Come on. Let's mingle."

"Roger and Hal! I haven't seen you since I was five foot three and two-hundred pounds. Remember me? Little Ricky Rickman?"

The guest who looked like he should be selling fine wines in a commercial laughed at the identical gap-mouthed reaction of his former classmates, two of the dozen or more males who had taunted him about his size when he was growing up. "No hard feelings, guys," he said, offering a sincere handshake.

"Ricky? What happened to you? I mean," Hal sputtered, "where did you go? One day you're there on the ballfield with us, huffing and puffing, trying to kick that damned soccer ball into the goal, and the next day – *poof*! – you're gone, and your locker and desk are empty."

"I would try to make you – and everyone else who went to that damned privileged academy – feel bad by saying I had a nervous breakdown, but the truth is, my dad got transferred to London. Once there, I really got into playing soccer, or as they call it, football. Plus, with only blood pudding and other traditional British food to eat, I stopped overeating and grew into my weight. I thank my lucky stars that Dad wasn't sent to Paris. Can you imagine what I'd look like if I had free range of all those French pastries?"

Roger and Hal laughed nervously at the image. The man before them was not only fit, he seemed to be the model of health for men in their sixties. Broad-shouldered and with thick hair that shone like polished silver – he was an Adonis for any age.

"I'm sorry," Roger said. "Not to be rude, but why are you here? I haven't seen you in generations. Literally!"

"My son and I were invited to your daughter's birthday party." He pulled out the invitation and showed it to Roger. "I thought it was a little unconventional, but when I saw your name on it, I decided we had to come and see if it was for real or a prank. It took a little arm-twisting on my part to get him here, but we made it."

Roger scanned the invitation, immediately disgusted that it had a provocative photo of his daughter printed on the inside. Draped in furs, she was leaning forward to show cleavage, wearing at least ten carats of diamonds and an uncomfortable smile that looked more like a pained grimace to him. He blinked back his disgust and read:

You are invited to Vickie Lynn Thornwhistle's Sixteenth Birthday Gala.

Meet the young lady who is heir to the largest distributor of fine arts on the east coast.

Take this opportunity to find out if your child is compatible with ours. A merger or joint venture might be in your son or daughter's future.

RSVP E. E. Swensen for Roger and Gloria Thornwhistle

"Didn't your wife tell you she had invited me? Oh, that's right. She may not have known we were acquainted when we were younger."

"First off, I had nothing to do with this tacky and tawdry invitation. Second, I'm sure my wife is also unaware of it. Third," Roger scanned the room for either a *doppelganger* to Rick or a short rotund boy, "you have a son here?"

"He's the young man speaking with the lady over there. Is *that* your wife?"

Hal and Roger followed Rick's nod that directed them to a tall, handsome young man listening to Nanny Elsa. Her face was shiny with nervous sweat, her hands flicking about, fidgeting with her hair, then landing on the guest's arm. "Her?" Roger squeaked. "My wife? Oh, good God, no!"

Hal didn't even try to contain his laugh but did bring the quick outburst down to a chuckle, earning a sneer from Roger.

Feeling the need for payback, Roger bent forward and squinted in her direction, pretending to focus on her face. "She's not mine, but isn't that *your* wife, Hal?" he asked, elbowing Hal in the ribs, flipping the joke back on him.

Hal growled at being punked, then shook his head and gave in to the levity. "If you don't remember, Rick, Roger and I are cousins. It must be all these youthful hormones in the air. I feel like I'm sixteen again. How old is your son?"

"Rich is twenty. He's attending Harvard. So, if she isn't your wife, do you know who she is? That woman seems to have an unnaturally keen interest in my son."

The three men watched in disgust as the skinny gray-haired crone moved her hand up and down Rich's arm seductively, the sly grin on her face followed by her tongue rimming her upper lip.

"I think I'm going to be ill..." Roger said. "Excuse me, Rick. It looks like your son's being quite the gentleman but enough is enough. He's in need of a rescue."

Hal reached out and held Rickman back. "Let him handle it. She's his daughter's nanny. That Swedish witch has been giving him fits for years. She may have just crossed the line with hitting on your son, though."

The younger Rickman squirmed uncomfortably under the hag's touch; her graphic description of her sexual skills unbelievable. "Excuse me," he said, tactfully removing the crazy old woman's grasp from his arm. "I think I'll have to pass. I think I see the guest of honor..."

Elsa's hand reached out and grabbed his, ready to bring it to her silicone-enhanced breast. "We can share the pleasures of my

Scandinavian..."

"Excuse me a moment," Roger said, stepping between the couple. An awkward three-way scuffle ensued as Rich disentangled himself from Elsa's clutch. As he backed away, she moved closer, trying for a more controlling hold, at the same time trying to nudge Roger out of the way.

Elsa became aware of the murmurs and realized she was desperately clinging to a man a third her age and let go. Her embarrassed slump-shouldered posture changed in a flicker to standing bold and upright; stoic and authoritative. "I hope you have a good reason for interrupting our conversation," she said, teeth clenched and eyes afire.

"Indeed, I do," he answered. "Rich, I see you've met my daughter's nanny. She's been around for," he sighed deeply, trying for the most caustic way to offend her without it making even more of a scene. "Well, let's just say that big oak tree was a cast aside acorn when she came to work for our family. Come, let me introduce you to my daughter, Vickie Lynn."

Elsa stuck her chest out, momentarily dumbstruck at Roger's nerve. By the time she thought of a scathing retort, her moment had passed. The men were already halfway across the room. *You'll pay for that, Mr. Moneybags. I don't take being cast as an aging servant lightly!*

"I don't think we've been introduced," Rich said, reaching out to shake Roger's hand. "Oh, and thanks for the rescue," he added in a whisper.

"Don't worry about it," he replied in the same tone, then spoke up. "I'm Roger Thornwhistle. Your father and I went to school together many, many years ago. I think the Longwood Academy is a museum now."

"Richard Othello Albert Rickman, the Third, but please call me Rich."

"Ooh." Roger resisted the urge to laugh out loud at the initials. "It's a good thing your father never used his middle names. We would have given him even more grief!"

"Me? I love it. I can't wait for someone to tease me. I won't do it here with all of your guests, especially since this is the first time I've met many of these people, but I have a wickedly loud roar. It works great at the fraternity parties."

"After everyone's had a few?" Roger prompted.

"Oh, yeah…" Rich mused, then blushed. If Roger had been getting reacquainted with his father, there was a good chance he knew he was underage for drinking.

Seeing the telltale signs of chagrin, Roger thumped him on the back. "Just don't drink around my daughter. As a reminder," he cleared his throat, "my daughter is only sixteen. I was only recently made aware that her nanny had invited so many older young men to her soiree."

"That's pretty good, Mr. Thornwhistle: two oxymorons in one sentence."

"Excuse me?"

"This event is way beyond what I'd call a soiree…"

"And?"

"Older young men," Rich said, his smile barely contained.

"*Touché.* I guess I'd better warn you, though. My daughter is not only sharp, but she's also beautiful. Don't go falling in love with her, all right?"

"Sir, I can't promise that, but I will promise to treat her like a lady and not take advantage of her."

"And?"

"What do you mean, 'and'?"

Roger thumped him on the back. "Don't let her talk you into anything crazy like taking advantage of *you*!" He took one step back and looked at the now red-faced Rich.

"Great. Just what I wanted to see. At least you had the common sense to blush at my remark. Good move. Remember it one of these days if you have a daughter of your own. It's a scary business, having one who's both clever and beautiful. I'd like to keep her down on the farm, so to say, until she's a little – or rather, a lot – more savvy about the tricks and tropes of the world and the people in it, but I don't think that's going to happen."

"I can appreciate wanting that. I have a sister who's fifteen years older than me. I was the surprise baby. She got suckered into rotten marriage at an early age. I can't imagine having to deal with a carousing husband and a baby at any age, much less at twenty and in a country so far away from our mother. I promise you, I'll treat your daughter with respect."

Roger realized that during their discourse, they had wound up in the kitchen, away from the other guests, and were now in the way of the serving staff. "Either you're a good man, ROAR the Third, or you're an excellent bullshit artist. Let's hope it's the former and not the latter."

Now it was Rich's turn to offer a hand. He set it on Roger's shoulder. "I'll tell you right now, I'm a lousy liar. Never learned how and was told it was a skill a gentleman didn't need. I haven't even seen your daughter but with a father like you, she at least had the opportunity to learn how to be a lady."

"Bullshit?" Roger asked with a wink.

"I'd prefer to think of this one as I'm a man who's a good judge of character. You see, *my* father was a great teacher, too."

The two made their way back into the main room. Guests were practically elbow-to-elbow, the extra dinner tables taking up the milling around area that was necessary for social gatherings. Suddenly, Roger felt a tug at his elbow.

"There you are," Vickie whispered harshly. "Mom's been looking everywhere for you. I think she's having a meltdown."

Roger's eyes widened as he searched the room for her. "Where?" he asked.

"She went to her room. You'd better get to her before you-know-who sends her over the edge."

"Excuse me," Roger said, remembering he was escorting Rich. "This is my daughter, Vickie Lynn…"

"Go, go, go!" Rich said. "We got this."

The young duo watched Roger weave through the groups of three and four guests, standing with drinks in hand, carrying on small talk to pass the time.

"Damned Elsa!" Vickie hissed. "It's all her fault."

"The nanny?" Rich asked.

"You must have met her."

Rich nodded and opened his mouth, ready to share at least a little of his experience and rescue but closed it, continuing to nod. He suddenly realized he hadn't been introduced. "Oh, I'm Rich, by the way..."

Before he could say another word, Vickie cut him off. "Rich? Yeah, you and every other man who's introduced himself to me this evening."

"Excuse me?"

"I'm sorry. That was crass, but I've had no less than six men approach me in the last fifteen minutes, pawing at my hand, telling me all about their portfolios and athletic prowess. I could care less about how many letters a guy got in college or whether he's new money, old money, or no money. Geez!"

Rich pulled out each pants pocket, showing they were empty. "No money," he said and smirked. "I'd show you my elephant impersonation, but I told your father I'd behave."

"Your what? Oh, my..." Grace's hand flew to her mouth to cover her laugh. "Oh, please do not show that!"

"And just for the record, my name is Rich as in Richard. I'd tell you my whole name, but then I'd have to give you my lion impersonation, too."

"What does your name have to do with a lion? Are you a Leonard?"

"No, but I was born in the house of Leo."

"Capricorn," Vickie said, her hands up to mime goat horns.

"I knew that."

"How?"

"Duh? Isn't this your birthday party?" Rich asked.

"Duh is right. I'm sorry. We got off on the wrong foot. I'm extremely ticked because I thought this was just going to be family and a few friends. Next thing I know, I'm being fitted for a dress Nanny Elsa ordered one size too small so 'I' would fit the dress, not the other way around. I'm so hungry, I could eat the buttons off your jacket."

Rich looked down at his tux, found the button and was ready to pop it off when he felt her hand on his. *Zing! Oh, my God! That really does happen!*

"It was a joke," Vickie said, her voice soft and sincere, bringing him back to reality. Harshness overtook her tone as she continued, "Elsa claims to be Swedish, but I swear she's an escaped Nazi. She doesn't want me to eat tonight – she thinks I'm still too fat. She's intolerable when I disobey her, so how about I sit next to you? It's a buffet. If you double-load your plate, I can sneak bites from it."

"You're only sixteen?" Rich asked, verifying that he should squelch the tingles he was getting for a minor.

"Yup. Remember that. And if you see me in a desperate situation and one of my crew doesn't catch on first, please come to my rescue."

"Your crew?"

She nodded to the threesome watching the two of them talk. "The youngest one is my unofficial godfather, Dusty. You already met my father. The balding one shooting daggers with his eyes is my father's cousin, Hal. I don't know who that silver-haired guy is. He looks familiar, though. I think I saw him on the cover of a magazine or something."

"Yup. That's my father, Rick Rickman. He's been on the cover of Forbes, Wine World, and a few others. We own a few acres of vineyards in Oregon. It looks like they're looking out for you."

"Yeah, well, they can only look so far," Vickie said, thinking of Nanny Elsa's privileged access to her when a man wasn't allowed in the room.

Sensing her gloom, Rich touched her elbow, wanting to reconnect and see if that *zing* was still there. *Zing!* Yup. She may be the one, but if so, he had to wait at least two years for her. Damned gypsy fortune teller! 'Two years of torment until she is yours' was right!

"Come on. Let's go eat," he said. "Chances are, you're suffering from malnutrition or at least low blood sugar. I don't want you passing out. The way those guys are looking at us, they'd blame me if you fainted."

Comforted by his touch, Vickie looked up at him and smiled, feeling at ease for the first time all day. "How tall are you?"

"Six-three in my bare feet." He lifted one foot and checked the heel. "Probably six-five in these. Why?"

"Tall, compassionate, and Rich. Any other attributes?" she asked, trying to compose herself. *Dang! Why did you ask? The tingles are just because you're hungry!*

"I didn't earn the height, and my parents gave me the name. I learned compassion by example, and my mother picked out the tux. Nope. I really don't have any attributes. I am the sum of my environment and genetics."

"Don't sell yourself short, tall boy. You could have resisted the clothing, chosen to go by a nickname, and ignored your parent's examples of compassion. I'd say your greatest attribute is making wise choices. Or at least good ones."

Rich chuckled then let go of her elbow and picked up a dinner plate. "I'll let you make the choices on food tonight. I'll eat just about anything." *I make wise choices? Yes, I choose you!*

***

The string quartet changed from dinner music to a waltz. "Care to dance with your old man?" Roger asked. "Or do you want to spend the whole evening with Rich?"

She looked down and blushed, then stood up. "Daddy…"

He led her to the dance area. "Sorry, I didn't mean to make you uncomfortable." He held one hand and placed the other on her waist, ready for the waltz. "Good Lord, girl! You're as skinny as a broom! Why haven't you been eating?"

Done protecting her, Vickie lifted her chin and declared with eyes squinted in barely contained rage, "Because Nanny Elsa says I'm too fat!"

"You are *not* fat," Roger hissed, returning the squint, then looking around the room for the tormentor. "That's it. I don't care what she has on us. She's getting fired."

"She has on us?" Vickie asked. "Has she been..."

Roger quickly put his hand on her mouth. "Don't say it, dear. Please, don't say a word. I shouldn't have lost my cool. You are the only thing in this world that matters to your mother and me. Truly. You have to know that we wouldn't have allowed her in this house for so long if it hadn't been for a good reason. Or at least a reason so profound that life itself wouldn't be worth living if we lost it. She threatened to have you removed. Poof. You would have been out of our lives if we didn't acquiesce to her demands."

"So, that's why you gave her your Maserati for Christmas last year?"

Roger nodded, his lips tight. "Please don't let your mother know I slipped. And please, for all the love you have for us, don't ask about what she's blackmailing us with."

"Daddy, I don't know and I don't care. All I want is for us to stay together as a family. Believe it or not, just knowing that she's using the 'B' word to keep her job makes me feel so much better. I thought it was because you and Mommy thought I needed correcting or changed or..."

"Sweetheart, you are and always have been perfect." He looked down at her bony shoulder. "Except for being too thin. I'll tell her I want you to start eating better, that I'm afraid you're suffering from bulimia or anorexia or whatever that disease is. If I ask her to make sure you overcome it, maybe she'll back off. At this point, all I can do is hope she tires of us. Or that she's extorted enough money and goods that she wants to start afresh in another country. Your Uncle

Hal seems to think Costa Rica is a great place to send wayward women. Maybe I should get her a one-way ticket for Valentines' Day?"

Roger felt a tap on his shoulder. He turned and saw Papa Doc. "Care to let a party crasher butt in?"

"Party crasher?" Roger asked. "I asked specifically that you and Silas be invited." His face reddened as he realized he had told Elsa. Obviously, she wanted complete control over the guest list. "Yes, as far as I'm concerned, you're one of her grandpas. Hal told me that his invitation was a verbal from my wife. Damned Swedish tyrant!"

"Now, now, Daddy," Vickie soothed. "Go fume somewhere else and let me dance with Papa Doc."

Roger looked up and saw Silas had joined Rick, Dusty, and Hal near the bar, the group swapping stories as they watched the birthday girl dance. "Sounds like a plan," he said, ceding the dance to Papa Doc.

"Good evening, Silas," Roger said as he joined the crew. "I apologize for the invitations not reaching you and Doc." Hal raised his hand. "And Hal, too," he added. "My life would be so much simpler – and my blood pressure so much lower – if I could just get rid of that damned Elsa."

Silas leaned over and whispered in Roger's ear. "Don't worry about it. Hal has me in the loop." He stood up straight and looked at Rick Rickman, a face he recognized from the trade magazines. "We finally meet. I think we've done a little negotiating over the last few years. Silas Priest," he said, reaching out and offering his hand.

"Priest?" Rickman repeated, obviously unfamiliar with the name but shaking hands just the same. "Silas... Oh, yes! Silas! You helped me find out about that manager who was trying to steal me blind about three, four years ago! Ah, great going. I don't know if you ever heard the rest of the story. I was able to recover all my funds. Silly ass. He put all the cash in a safety deposit box then mailed the key to himself at the office. I was given a heads up and able to intercept it. Because it had the company name and his job

49

title on it, I had full legal rights to take it. I kicked him to the curb and sent him on his way. No lawyers required."

"Yeah, I thought you'd like that. He thought I was doing him a favor, telling him to liquidate all his assets into cash, send them to a spot no one would suspect, and then grab it and hightail it out of the country," Silas said, laughing as he recalled the clueless embezzler.

"Excuse me, just a minute," Hal said, his hand on Roger to get his attention. "Did you tell Vickie Lynn to get her ears fixed?"

"Fixed?" Roger asked, then watched as his daughter danced with Papa Doc, waiting for her to turn so he could see.

"Shit! That tyrant! I'll bet Elsa is behind that. Vickie couldn't have had it done without an adult signing a consent form. I gave that bitch medical power of attorney when we first hired her. If something happened while they were at the park, I wanted to make sure she could receive medical treatment. Damn her eyes!"

Dusty and Hal both took a step forward, looking for Elsa. "Hold on there, guys," Silas said, physically restraining them. "Remember. This is Vickie Lynn's party. The deed has been done. No undoing it now. You don't want her to remember her sixteenth birthday party as the one..."

"Ah, crap!" Dusty said.

"Go ahead and say it, son," Hal said, seeing the same thing that had raised Dusty's ire.

"Ah, shit!" Dusty hissed, feeling better for losing his social filter.

The melody of Strauss's Blue Danube fell apart as two of the string quartet moved out of the way of the skinny crone who was backing into them, under verbal attack by a very irate Grace Rhodes.

"Her ears were perfect, you bitch! How dare you make her feel bad about her image. And I heard how you've browbeaten her into believing she's fat..."

Elsa picked her way around the violinist, standing behind his chair for protection from the angry godmother. "She'll never get a good husband with those Dumbo ears and pot belly!" Elsa hissed, then moved in front of the seat, no longer afraid. The crowd would be on her side. "I was doing her a favor."

Thunk!

Humph!

A quick punch to the gut and Elsa was bent over at the waist, the wind knocked out of her.

Grace looked around the room, suddenly aware that she had not only lost her temper but had struck out in anger. Dusty was standing next to Hal – her husband and father both wide-eyed. In a blink of an eye, they were grinning, transitioning from shock to glee at the same rate.

"Watch out!" a woman's voice called out.

Grace heard the whoosh of a punch being thrown and stepped back in reflex.

"You bitch," Elsa huffed with the missed blow. Still winded, the angry nanny held her hands up, ready for a boxing match, then realized the room was full of rich and influential guests. She looked up and saw that every one of them was slack-jawed in shock.

Fwap! Fwap!

"Never take your eyes off your opponent," Grace hissed. "And if you ever touch my daughter again, I'll gut you and use your liver for dog food."

"Your daughter?" Elsa asked, a glimmer of inspiration sparkling her otherwise glazed eyes.

Fwap!

The final blow – an open-handed slap – sent Elsa to the ground in a pile of sequins and snot, a trickle of blood mixing with the dribble of makeup sliding off her face. Hairpiece askew, her upper plate of false teeth had slid halfway out of her mouth. A perfect picture of retribution.

Grace looked up and saw Vickie clinging to the tall young man she had been eating dinner with. "Sorry, honey. Well… not really," she told her.

Vickie started giggling, a pensive nervous reaction at first, then winding up to the full laughter of absolute glee. "Well, you did say maybe someone would bash her for my birthday. Best sixteenth birthday present ever!"

Chapter 4: Birthday Bash

Rich grimaced at the emotional and physical spectacle but remained silent and supportive of the giddy teenager at his side, her boisterous laughs now settled down to intermittent chuckles. He didn't know the family dynamics but was uncomfortably acquainted with the tawdry and disgusting Nanny Elsa, now laid out on the parquet floor. She more than likely deserved the blows. Still, it was Vickie's birthday. "Shall we make the rounds and see if we can provide a little damage control?" he asked, urging the birthday girl away.

"Ooh, that was *rich*," she said with a giggle, indicating the rout but teasing him about his name. She quickly sobered up, realizing she didn't want to embarrass her parents with even more rowdy behavior. "Sorry about the tussle," she said sincerely. "That's been a long time coming."

"She probably deserved it," he said, nudging her upper arm-to-shoulder with body language that said, 'That's okay. I'm cool with it.'

She leaned into him and looked up. "Yes, that was very rich. No doubt the guests will remember this night for years."

"Yes, and now everyone will want to come to your parties. You can't hire that kind of excitement."

The young couple stood back and watched as Silas ushered in three valets to help lift the aging pugilist from the floor to her feet. As she regained consciousness, Nanny Elsa's arms flailed, resisting the assistance offered, her striking-out protests prolonging the performance. The hag was leaving the humiliation spotlight but not the partygoer's memories.

Silas drew out his handkerchief and made a quick swipe of the mess on the floor, dropped his improvised rag into a plastic bag he took from his pocket, then followed the group. *Now, who are you really, Nanny Elsa? A little DNA research might help. By the time I get the results back, you'll probably still be hanging around, your claws into someone else in this household or neighborhood. Six months is a long time to wait for lab results. Let's just hope I find out something from other sources sooner.*

On the other side of the room, Dusty and Hal came to Grace's side, chatting nonsense to keep her from watching the staff remove the fallen Elsa. "Dad, why don't you go see how Roger's holding up?" Dusty suggested, his quick eye movements letting him know he needed some private time with his wife.

"Don't worry, honey," Dusty said once they were alone. "Papa Doc made sure she didn't have any serious injuries. He called an ambulance just to cover our asses in case she decides to get litigious. I don't think the guests saw it as anything but self-defense. Actually, people seem to be having a good time now. At least they have something to talk about."

Young Rich stood off to the side, waiting silently for a break in their conversation. "I think Vickie wants to talk to you alone," he said when Grace noticed him. "She has something for you in the kitchen."

Grace looked back at Dusty. He shook his head and shrugged. "Don't look at me," he said. "You know that girl has a mind of her own."

An anxious Vickie waited at the breakfast bar for Grace. Starting to chew on her cuticle, she realized what she was doing and quickly brought her hand down and began twiddling her thumbs instead. When she heard Grace clear her throat, she stood up, making a concerted effort to keep her hands still.

"Hey, Grace," Vickie said, her arms crossed in front of her chest, hands tucked under her armpits. "Papa Doc said you should soak your hand in warm water and Epsom salts. I had the cook help me. I already had the Epsom salts. She just filled the big ceramic bowl with warm water. She said it's her favorite bread-making bowl; that it should keep the heat in longer than a stainless steel one. She said she'd do anything for you now. Everyone knows…"

"You're babbling, Vickie," Grace said, sitting down next to her.

54

She put her right hand in the water, an unintentional 'Ooh' escaping at the comforting warmth.

Vickie leaned closer to the bowl and sniffed. "I don't think it makes a difference if they're scented salts or not. You'll smell like roses for a while, though." Vickie realized that now she was rubbing her thumb and forefinger together, another form of thumb-twiddling that she'd seen her godmother do hundreds of times over the years.

Grace watched her mimic her nervous habit, then looked up at her with one eyebrow raised. 'What did you want to talk about?' she asked without saying a word.

"I just wanted to thank you in private for the greatest birthday present ever," Vickie blurted out.

Grace chuckled. "We both got a gift with that one. Turn around and let me look at your ear."

Vickie carefully lifted her fall of curls, exposing the infected area that Elsa had smeared with a heavy application of cover-up, trying to hide the red inflammation.

"Oh, good Lord," Grace exclaimed just a little too loudly.

Dusty stepped in from the hallway. "Is everything all right in here?"

"Go get Papa Doc. He needs to clean this up. He has his medical kit in the car. He won't leave home without it."

Vickie waited until Dusty was out of earshot to speak. "Grace?" she asked, her voice soft and pensive. She waited until Grace was looking right at her to continue. "Why did you say I was your daughter?"

Grace blanched. Had she really said that? Out loud? "Oh? I said that?" she answered, her eyes blinking rapidly as she watched the doorway to see if anyone had heard.

"Yes, you did." Vickie reached up and pulled back Grace's hair, exposing one ear.

"Ooh, that's cold," Grace said and shook her hair back in place, feeling naked and exposed at being inspected, certain that Vickie had noticed that their ears were the same. Or were before the procedure.

"So, why did you say that?" Vickie persisted, not ready to let go of the suspicion she'd had since her thirteenth birthday.

"Well, you are my daughter," Grace said with a sudden surge of confidence. "You're my goddaughter, even if that's not a legal relationship."

"That must be why our ears look so much alike."

Grace chuckled, then – almost as an afterthought – said, "Yes, that's it."

"Funny. That's not what they told us in biology. Ear shape and pinnae are passed down from mother to daughter and father to son. That genetic trait is an even stronger and more direct indicator of relationship than hair or eye color."

The blood drained from Grace's face. "Really?" she asked, suddenly feeling as if she was going to faint.

Vickie laughed nervously, unsure if she wanted to continue talking about her suspicion or not. Her compassion got the best of her when she saw how upset Grace was. "Maybe it's true. I don't know. I just made that up. What I *do* want to know is why you looked like I just caught you in a lie when I said that..."

"Did someone call for a doctor?" Papa Doc called in from the hallway, Dusty standing behind him.

Dusty sat down beside Grace and looked at Papa Doc. *Do you feel it?*

Yes, I feel the tension in the room, too. That's why I was so bright and boisterous when I came in – to give the women a chance to recover their composure.

"I already had the bag with me. Looks like you're doing all you can for that hand, Grace." Papa Doc sniffed the air. "Tea or Damask roses?"

"Damask," Vickie said. The two women looked at each other and blinked, a visual agreement that they'd continue their conversation later – without anyone else around. Then Grace gave her a narrow-eyed maternal admonition and nodded, telling her to

56

show Papa Doc her infected ear.

Turning around as directed, Vickie pivoted in her seat and pulled back her hair.

Papa Doc frowned, then looked at the back of her other ear. "Well, at least only one of them is botched. Sorry, that sounds crude. Who did this?"

"The surgeon at Silver Falls Dermatology," Vickie said. "Nanny Elsa insisted he was the best."

"He's a damned butcher!" Papa Doc hissed, then composed himself. "That's not what I'm talking about, though. Who put on all this makeup? This is still a new wound. It needs fresh air and to be kept clean in order to heal properly. Don't worry. Your ear isn't going to fall off, but it may scar now. Well, first things first. I need to clean out this crud so it can heal right. Skin can't mend around foreign material. This is going to hurt, darling. Sorry, but I don't carry Lidocaine with me."

Papa Doc looked around the room. Grace was holding Vickie's hand and Dusty was standing in the doorway next to Ricky Rickman's kid – what was his name? – both frowning in concern. "Dusty, go get her a drink."

"Wine or champagne?"

"Neither. Whiskey. And make that two; one for her and one for me when I'm done. I sure hate to hurt my little girl, but it has to be done."

Papa Doc took out the jewel-encrusted comb from Vickie's hair and poked and scooted it, trying to find a way to keep his work area free from wayward curls.

"Here, let me help you," Grace said. With practiced skill, she inserted the comb with one-handed dexterity as he held the tress up, the two of them working as one. "You only had sons, so you probably never had to fix hair."

"Nothing more than a buzz cut in the summer when we were at the cabin."

"Thanks. And it may not be your birthday," Vickie said, then mouthed the word, 'Mom,' to Grace, "but it looks like you got a gift, too. I just hope she leaves and never comes back."

"That would be a gift to your whole family!" Papa Doc said, ending the remark with a snort of finality.

"Did I miss something?" Dusty asked, a drink in both hands.

"Nope," Grace said, all smiles at the prospect of the truth possibly coming out. "All's good here. Very good."

***

"All done," Papa Doc said. "Now, no hair product or spray perfumes or makeup or…"

"Got it. Keep the area free from anything but soap and water and this antiseptic."

"Yes, and just a dab. I'll be by in a day or two to check on you."

"Excuse me," Rich said, waiting in the doorway. "I have some good news. Or at least, I think it's pretty interesting."

"Shoot!" Dusty said.

"The party guests took a poll. Everyone here saw this fine woman," he nodded to Grace, "duck from a direct assault from Nanny Elsa. If said fine woman…"

"Her name is Grace," Hal said, now joining the group.

"Ah, the perfect name for her," Rich commented. "If Grace did throw the first punch, no one here tonight saw it. It would be the Swedish Serpent's word against everyone here."

"I'll say it again," Vickie held up her empty whiskey glass and toasted the group, "best birthday ever!"

***

"Are you sure you're all right?" Roger asked his daughter for the tenth time. Or so it seemed.

"Yes, I'm fine. I have a little bit of a headache but getting a full night's sleep should help that. Are you sure they're keeping Nanny Elsa overnight for observation?"

"I insisted on it," Roger said. "Even if she wanted to come back, I have a little bit of say there at that hospital. Plus, Silas is hanging around, asking questions. He has his way of getting informationthe."

58

"Like maybe if she's on pain medication, she'll answer anything he asks?"

"I always knew you were a clever girl," Roger said.

"Just like my daddy," she answered automatically, just as she always did when he complimented her on anything. She gasped as she realized he probably wasn't her bio-dad. Then she smiled. Yes, but he was her daddy.

He gave her a kiss on the cheek. "Now, get some sleep. It's been a long and exciting day."

"That's for sure. You and Mom get some sleep, too. I worry about both of you."

"Don't. It's all under control. Probably now more than ever."

"Night, night."

Vickie waited until she heard his footfalls disappear, then stepped into the hallway to verify. *Yup. Gone to the other side of the house. Perfect. Now to do a little Silas-style snooping of my own.*

She had always been curious about what Nanny Elsa kept in her room. She had never been allowed in there. She had seen, though, where the not-as-clever-as-she-thought nanny kept her spare key. Vickie reached under the drawer on the vase table and felt around. *Yes!* The key was hers now.

The room wasn't dirty or messy, but it was crowded with neatly stacked boxes, all labeled with letters and numbers that meant nothing to her. The only area that was uncluttered was the bed and the desk. She ignored the bed. The thought of that woman in bedclothes – or less – turned her stomach. The desk was as intriguing as the box must have been to Pandora.

A pale-blue canvas journal with leather corners was set out, a ribbon trailing out the top as a bookmark. Vickie opened it and looked inside.

It wasn't a journal as in a diary, but a ledger. Columns of dates and commodities lined the one side, item numbers off to the right. Vickie glanced back at the cardboard boxes. Nanny Elsa had been accumulating goods not only from her parents – their names and dates were the most frequent on the listing – but from other people, too. She looked over the item names, printed out in a hand that was as clear as a computer font. The last journal entry was only two weeks ago:

12 December 2007. Thornwhistle Family hair comb: diamonds, rubies, sapphires. Under the column labeled value was marked: *est. $1,200,000.* The last column marked notes read: *Verify with jeweler.*

Item after item. Some were small such as *Merriweather Day Spa – the works – $800.* Others were obscure, like *15 January 1998 – New Bodyworks – Lap-Band – $40,000.* And some were just plain irritating. *5 December 2008 – 1992 Maserati Ghibli AM336 – est $75,000 – Note: intended 16th birthday gift VLT.*

"That bitch!" Vickie hissed. "Daddy was going to give me the Ghibli, but she blackmailed him for it."

Vickie thumbed through assorted papers – receipts and appraisals – that were in the back of the ledger and found what she was looking for: the title for her car. *"Voila!"* She rolled it into a tube and stuffed it down the back of her pajama bottoms. "Happy birthday to me all over again."

In the back of the ledger was an envelope with postal money orders in it. Uncashed ones from someone named Chuck Armstrong. "Papa Doc?" She thumbed through them. They were all made out to Gloria Thornwhistle and were from years past – some of them fifteen years ago. No, not Papa Doc. His name was A.B.C. Armstrong. Chuck was his son who'd been incommunicado for just about forever. But why was he sending money to her mother? And why did Nanny now have the checks? They had certainly expired by now. She looked at the post office stamp of where the latest one had been issued. Wolf Whistle, West Virginia in June 2005. At least it was a starting point.

Careful to cover any evidence of her snooping, Vickie set everything back in place including the spare room key taped to the drawer. Everything except the title to the Ghibli. She'd loved that car since the day her daddy first brought it home, all silver and shiny. *One day this is going to be yours*, he promised. And he was right.

Back in the privacy of her bedroom, she pulled out the paper and looked it over in brighter light. Her father had signed it over but hadn't written in the name of the new owner. His signature looked odd, though. It took a moment to realize what it was. He had dented the document from writing so hard. Stress. Duress. He hadn't wanted to do it.

Vickie looked at the bed. She wasn't the least bit tired. It was just the opposite. She was supercharged with a purpose. Exploratory energy was surging. Her suspicion that Grace was her biological mother just became more certain with her rock 'em, sock 'em, knock-down fight and the slip of the tongue at the party. She had also found out that her parents had been blackmailed for years. By whom was obvious: Nanny Elsa. The real question was 'why'? Daddy had said they didn't want to lose their little girl. Could Elsa have found out that Chuck Armstrong had proof she was adopted and she was tracking him? Did her parents actually think that she would choose *anyone* over them, even Dusty and Grace? They all got along: why would she want to change her family dynamics? Well, except for Nanny Elsa, everything was perfect. Time to get rid of her.

Rummaging through her closet, Vickie found some comfortable workout clothes and a warm jacket. She hadn't found the key to the Ghibli in the desk. It had to be in the key box in the garage with the other cars. She grabbed her backpack, gloves, and a scarf. Time for a ride!

***

Vickie strode into the garage with confidence and walked smack into a big, muscular someone.

"Whoa! What are you doing here?" Rich asked, reaching out to steady her.

"I live here," she said, stumbling backward. "What are you still doing here?"

"You don't live in the garage. I'm here because I had a couple of drinks with Hal and the guys. They offered me a place to stay for the night, but my truck has a big back seat. Plus, they'd have to run me back here in the morning. Not that I didn't want to see you again, but I didn't want to be a burden to them." Rich looked at her attire and noticed she had a backpack, ready to hit the road. "Are you driving or hitching a ride?" he asked.

"Huh?"

He pointed to the bag. "Two in the morning, a packed bag, warm coat, sneaking into the garage... I'd say it looks like you're running away."

"I'm not running away. I left a note. Well, I was going to. Once I got out here," she added sheepishly.

"Which car are you taking?" Rich asked, looking over the eight assorted types of vehicles.

"I'm taking mine. The Ghibli," she said, chin stuck out in defiance. "And I don't have to tell you anything. I just told you that because you'd know when I drove it out anyhow."

"Can't let you do it," Rich said, arms crossed in front of his chest, a sly smile on his face.

"You can't stop me," she said, her voice controlled, attitude determined.

"Well, I am bigger and stronger than you. And I did tell your father I wouldn't let you get into trouble. Or something like that. Besides, if you just turned sixteen today, you probably don't have your driver's license."

"I have my learner's permit."

"Yeah, well, you have to have another driver in the car for that to work. I don't see one around."

"You'll do. Come on. Let's go."

"Whoa! Whoa!" Rich uncrossed his arms and took two long strides to stand in front of her. "I can't go anywhere with you."

"Why not?"

"You're underage. I'm not. I'd get busted for... Well, it's pretty much illegal for anyone to take you anywhere without your parent's permission. Where are you headed at two in the morning? Why don't you wait until daylight and go with someone else? Lord knows you have enough people who care about you."

"How about you?"

"You're going to make me crazy, woman. I just told you…"

"Well, if you won't take me where I want to go, would you do me a favor?"

"Like what?"

"Take me to your place…"

"Nope. Still underage."

"Not that. What I want is to move my car off this property to somewhere Nanny Elsa won't find it. I'll bet my studded earrings that you have friends or family in the area where we can park the Ghibli."

Rich rolled his eyes. It was a *very* nice ride. He'd wanted one for years. With Maseratis, older was better, too. "Five miles down the road is my uncle's place. He has a big garage with lots of classics in it. We could probably slip another one in. But if you don't own this, you're stealing it. That's grand theft auto. That comes with more than a scowl and a slap on the hand."

Vickie opened up her backpack and pulled out the title. She had filled in her name as the buyer and backdated it to two days earlier. "See. I got it the day before my birthday."

"All right. Do you think you can follow me down the road? If you don't speed or weave all over the place, you shouldn't be pulled over and asked for your license. One question, though. Why do you want to move it? I'd be taking a big chance – or putting my uncle in a lurch – if your dad reports it stolen and it's found at his place."

Vickie didn't answer right away, her lips working back and forth as she thought of a good excuse.

"You know, I may be a lousy liar, but that doesn't mean I can't tell when someone else is lying to me," Rich said sarcastically.

"I didn't lie. I didn't say anything!"

63

"Yes, but you were thinking about what to say, and it wasn't the truth. Just tell me. What's the worst that can happen?"

"Nanny Elsa was trying to steal it from my father. Steal it through blackmail. He said it was my sixteenth birthday present and it is. I just can't keep it here until she's gone. She won't be back tonight, but they might – probably will – let her out of the hospital tomorrow. I don't want it here when she gets back. She wouldn't know it's missing for a long time anyhow because it's more of a summer car. It's usually stored in the garage all winter."

"Now see? Wasn't that easier? I can believe that's the truth. So, I see you have gloves. Leave a note and we can be on our way."

"You believe me?"

"Did you lie?"

"No."

"Okay, let's go."

Vickie grabbed the key out of the lockbox, scribbled, "I'll be back soon. Love ya, Dad & Mom!" on the dry erase board next to it, then got in the Ghibli. *As you always told me, Dad: soon is relative!*

Rich hit the button and waited for the garage door to open. "You go first. Wait until I get my truck out, and then follow me."

Haltingly at first, Vickie backed out. *Don't blow it, woman! Reverse is just like going forward, except exactly opposite.*

Rich rolled his eyes at her inexperience behind the wheel. Daddy probably always backed it out for her. She should make it down the road to Uncle Phil's house without a problem, though. The roads were dry and well-lit.

Rich added a scribbled postscript note to her quick 'See ya later' message and included his cellphone number, then backed his truck out. After making sure she was still following him, he pulled out his phone and dialed.

"Roger? Yeah, I know it's late. I'm glad you gave me your card. Vickie has the Maserati and is bringing it to my Uncle Phil's place up the road. Yeah, she said something about Nanny Elsa and making sure it was out of her clutches or something like that. Just don't go filing a stolen vehicle report. She has the title and it's signed over to her. I don't know your signature, but everything looked to be in order. I figure I'll let her do her thing, and then bring her back to your place in my truck. No, believe me, I know she's underage. I'd rather cut off my right arm than bother her! Yeah, well, if I didn't escort her, she'd be off on her own to parts unknown, ripe for trouble with whoever found her. She may be smart, but she's also good-looking and has an expensive car. She's a target for every flimflam man and Romeo on the east coast. I'll keep in touch. She doesn't know I'm contacting you, so let's keep it that way. And hey! Thanks for trusting me. That means a lot. See ya!"

Chapter 5: On the Road

January 4, 2008
3:30 AM

"Are you sure it's okay to leave it here? I'm sorta rethinking this. I still have to go someplace before Nanny Elsa gets out of the hospital and that's my only ride."

"How far? Can we be back before anyone knows you're missing?" Rich asked. "I'll drive."

Vickie took the map out of the console and opened it up. *Where in the hell is Wolf Whistle, West Virginia? I can already tell he's not going to let me go anywhere by myself. The key is in the locked dropbox now, so I can't get it back. Damn!* "Hmm. We're here and I want to go south."

"That's what you said. What I'm wondering is how far south. What's the name of the town?" *She's stalling. She doesn't know where she's headed. Fine. I have plenty of fuel. I'll play along for two hours, and then I'm hauling her back to Daddy. Hopefully, not kicking and screaming, but back to her parents, just the same.*

"Woodstock."

"New York? There's no way…"

"No, Woodstock, Connecticut."

"I know where that is, but it's east of here, not south."

"Oh, I must be holding the map upside down."

"All right, we'll go. But you try and get some rest. You get to drive us back home. Do you think you can handle this beast?"

"Um, what beast?" Vickie asked, blushing because she had been staring at the five o'clock shadow on his face. Or three A.M. shadow.

"This three-quarter-ton truck. Here. We'll find out soon enough. Use my coat as a pillow."

Rich reached behind the seat, grabbed his denim and sheered-wool jacket, and handed it to her. His spread-arm movement scented the air with male musk and fatigue, a faint hint of leftover cologne adding a spicy tang to the aromatherapy that made her lady parts tingle.

"Okay," she said, hoping she didn't sound as breathless as she felt, "I'll try to sleep. It's been a wild and crazy twenty-four hours."

Rich cranked up the fan on the heater. "Yeah, well, I certainly didn't see me taking an underage woman across state lines in the wee hours of the morning, either," he said, then realized that he had just said that aloud.

"Hmm?" she asked, snuggling into the soft, fleecy interior of his coat that smelled like her hero.

"Nothing. Just get some sleep."

Two hours later, the weary driver pulled into the all-night diner. The thunk-thunk of the truck passing over the curb and sudden absence of road noise awakened the damsel on her mission of discovery. "Wait. Where are we?" she asked, biting off the next question of, 'And who are you?' as she realized who he was: her gallant knight, escorting her on her quest.

Her smile of contentment widened. What he didn't know was that her final destination was West Virginia. Even if she couldn't find it on the printed road map, someone along the way was sure to have heard of Wolf Whistle!

"I have to stop for coffee and something to eat. You could use a big breakfast, too," Rich said, his voice rough and dry. He swallowed and tried to clear his throat, but the noise came out lusty – sounding more like an invitation to foreplay than a search for spittle. "And I need water, lots of water. The heater dried me out."

Click. Vickie unbuckled, leaning forward as she wiggled away from his coat. "You need this more than I do now."

Rich stared at her breasts bouncing around an arm's reach away… "No," he said, his voice now even lower and more guttural. Primal. "On second thought," he said, and pulled it onto his lap. "I'll meet you inside. Gotta get fuel." He shifted in his seat, moving aside his early morning discomfort, glad he had the jacket for cover in case she looked over.

"All right. Oh, and thanks. You're a great white knight. Well, all the white knights were the good guys but you're great. I guess they were all white, too – as in Caucasian – back in the feudal days of England. Oh, ignore me. I haven't had coffee yet and I'm rambling," Vickie said and opened the door, trying to leave the truck with at least a little dignity.

But, you're so cute when you babble! Rather than try and speak without a full voice again, Rich gave her a two-fingered wave of farewell. He paused before heading to the gas pumps and pretended to look for something in the console, waiting to make sure she entered the café. *Two years until you're eighteen... Two years from now, will you be even more intriguing? 'Two years of torment until she is yours.' Double-damn you, gypsy!*

"Hey, Roger! It's me, Rich. Sorry, my voice is shot. We're in Connecticut. I'm stopping for fuel and breakfast. I think this short trip will get her grounded to reality. Yeah, I know she's just a kid. She's on some quest for a unicorn or justice or something. Sorry. I need coffee. Just checking in. She's fine. Yeah, well, I'm hoping she calls you. Text me if she does. She's a good kid. Yes, yes, I know she's still a kid. Hey, the gas guy's here. Talk to you later. *Click.*

"How did I get myself into this?"

***

All fueled up and ready for coffee, Rich entered the small Mom and Pop restaurant. Momentary panic buckled his knees as he searched the room and didn't see her.

Vickie came out of the 'His and Hers' bathroom that was located right behind him and stood quietly, watching him search for her. When she realized that his level of concern wasn't irritation but terror, she decided to stop tormenting him.

"Looking for me?" she asked, a slight smile of mischief brightening her eyes.

He spun around, an audible gasp of relief escaping. "Who else would I be looking for?" he said, his voice raspy as a baseball fan after a double-header, his emotions mixed with frustration and joy. Seeing a table already set for the next customer, he took the glass of water and guzzled it down with a quick glug-glug. "Let's sit here," he said, his voice rehydrated and back to near normal. "I'll be right back."

The weary driver, still attired in formal dinner clothes less the tuxedo jacket, stopped at the checkout counter and souvenir shop. A pair of U Conn sweatpants and a long-sleeved tee that read 'Woodstock: Still a great place to be' would draw less attention to a man escorting a female minor. While waiting for the cashier to ring up his sale, he overheard an older man pause his walker at their table and address Vickie.

"Good morning, Ria. How's your dad doing?"

Knowing that he couldn't be talking to her, Vickie continued to read the 'Stuff you didn't know about Connecticut' advertisement and trivia flyer that was on the table.

"Hmph!" the senior muttered and continued to the cash register, frustrated that he had been ignored.

"Hey, Alice," he said when he got to the cashier. "What's Ria doing in here without Doc? Her old man never lets her go anywhere by herself. Plus, she ain't old enough to drive yet."

"Are you sure that's her?" Alice asked, looking around Rich to get a better view. "Nah. There's a definite similarity, but Ria's not that skinny. This one looks half-starved."

The old man nodded in agreement. "Yeah, plus she doesn't have those cute little elf ears like Ria. Damned if they don't look enough alike to be twins, though."

Rich took his change, headed into the restroom, then opened the door again quickly, looking back at their table to make sure she hadn't taken off in his truck. He shook his head, trying to clear the brain fog of fatigue. She couldn't do that. He still had the keys. He splashed water on his face. That helped a little, but what were those locals saying about her being a twin? They didn't know that she'd had her ears 'fixed.' He only knew because that was the reason why her godmother had pummeled Nanny Elsa.

That's a mother's defensive move, not a godmother's. And if I have this figured out right, Vickie is chasing down clues about what her nanny has been blackmailing her parents with. Could it be that the Thornwhistles adopted a twin and this Ria is the other one? Grace does look enough like Vickie to be her mother. Crap. I gotta eat and get some sleep. Maybe if I could see this Ria, I'd know. Something is up if she really does look like Vickie's twin.

Rich approached the cashier after he came out, dressed as a tourist or local, not a hungover partier. "Excuse me," he said. "I have a little problem I wanted to see a doctor about before I got further down the road. Is there one around here?"

"Yup. Doc has a clinic a ways outside of town. Not that this is much of a town, but he likes being remote. He thinks city air isn't good for him and his daughter. That doesn't stop him from coming in and getting a nice stack of blueberry pancakes and a side of bacon once a month or so. Here. Let me draw you a map. He doesn't take appointments. 'Just show up when you're ailing,' he says."

"Sounds like my kind of man." Rich watched the gnarled hands draw a simple map on the back of a paper placemat. "Just tell him Alice sent you. Not that it'll get you a discount. He just asks folks to pay what they feel his time is worth. If they can't afford that, they usually work out something with jams and jellies or knit caps and afghans. He's pretty easy going."

"Thanks. I think I'll give him a little time, though. It's still pretty early. My cousin and I were just passing through on our way back from a big shindig in Massachusetts. Silly me. I totally forgot to bring a change of clothes. A plate of pancakes and side of bacon with a double-strength cup of coffee sounds great. She should know what she wants to eat by now, too."

"Be right there," she said.

"Hey, Cuz," Rich said as he slid into the booth.

"Cuz?" Vickie asked softly.

"Hey, cousins are fine to be traveling with," he whispered

across the table. "Remember, I could get in a lot of trouble just being with you. Give me a little alibi or validation or something, okay? Now, what do you want to eat?"

"I'm not hungry."

"I don't know if you even know what hungry is anymore. You're shivering because you don't have a calorie to burn for heat. While you're with me, I want you to eat. And I don't mean just move your food around on your plate and pretend, either. I'll order for you."

"No, that's okay. I'll have an egg white and mushroom omelet, no cheese."

"Bullshit."

"Ew! That would taste terrible with eggs." Vickie sneered, then burst out laughing.

"Pancakes and bacon with coffee and an orange juice," Rich said.

"That's too much," Vickie started to protest.

"That's for me."

"Oh. Dang. That sounded pretty good."

Rich looked up and saw the cashier, now his waitress, marking on her notepad. "Double that order except you know how I want my coffee."

"Sure thing, Cuz," she said with a wink.

***

"I can't believe I ate half of that pancake and three pieces of bacon."

"It was only one pancake, even if it did fill half the plate. So, on another subject, where are we going? I mean, why are we going?"

"I want to find out what Elsa's holding over my parents' heads. I know that comb she said was her family heirloom has been in my father's family for generations and was going to be mine. I guess she didn't know that I knew, or she wouldn't have tried to tell me such a bodacious lie. And the Ghibli! Dad bought that just after I was born. It was our summer touring vehicle. She knew that I knew, too, because she's been my nanny since before I was old enough to read. While she was gone, I snooped in her room. I found her ledger of ill-gotten gains. It lists everything she's taken, who she took it from and when, and its estimated value. That woman could probably buy a villa in France if she wanted. Why would she stick around?"

"Greed."

"Huh?"

"Greed. Plain and simple. She wants more. It's a sickness. I see a lot of it. Mr. A. has a home with ten bedrooms and twelve baths, so Mr. B. thinks he needs one with fourteen of each. Mrs. C. has a three-carat diamond ring, so Mrs. D. wants three-and-a-half carats. Truth is, one bedroom per person in the house is plenty, and it's only tradition that says a wedding ring is even necessary."

"Yeah, diamonds aren't for everyone," Vickie said with a snort. "They seem to get some people in trouble. Hence the hair comb Elsa extorted from my dad."

"Yes, but will you feel the same way when you find the man you want to marry? What would you do if he didn't offer you a great big chunk of ice to show off to your friends?"

Vickie looked up and sneered, her head shaking back and forth slowly. "You certainly don't know me. Just because I grew up entitled doesn't mean that I feel I deserve it all. I'll get my education, and then go out in the world and make a difference. Having the biggest house or more diamonds means nothing to me. Having parents who don't look like they're afraid of losing me or each other, is. I'm not on this quest for goods or money. I'm out to spare my parents."

"How are you going to do that?"

"The way I figure it, there's some sort of information Elsa is holding over them. If I find out what it is, then I can – how would you say? – deflate or devalue that tidbit. Blackmail is about words or pictures being withheld. I want to make that information worthless."

"You're pretty smart for your age, Cuz," Rich said, adding a wink.

"Must run in the family. Now, let's pay up and hit the road. We have a long way to go."

"About that," Rich said, adding a fake wince of pain. "Where is our final destination? You said Woodstock and we're here now."

"How far are you willing to go? I mean, it really is south of here."

"In for a penny, in for a pound."

"It's a little place called Wolf Whistle, West Virginia..."

Rich gasped in shock, then turned it into a groan. "I hate to cut this trip short, but I have to go see a doctor before we go too much further. I got a...a..."

Quick, think of a disease. She doesn't have a brother, so make up something male-related.

"I got a man-type problem. Something I need to talk to a doctor about. I asked about one when I came in, just in case. I was hoping it would get better if I ate, but it's still there. Come on. Let's go."

"But..."

"It won't take long. Just a little side trip. He probably has some medicine that will help. It's not something you can get over the counter, though."

Opening her mouth to protest again, Vickie realized that she was stuck. At his mercy. She couldn't go anywhere without him. Whether there really was such a thing as a 'man-type' problem that could be cured by a doctor's special potion or not, she'd have to give in just a little. At least he wasn't trying to hit on her. *Dang it!*

"Are you okay to drive? I mean, just tell me where we're going..."

"I'll drive. I got the directions before we ate, just in case. It won't take too long."

"But you don't have an appointment." Vickie suddenly paled. Was he going to take her into the woods and rape her? Had she really made such a rash decision? How stupid was she to be taking off with someone she'd just met, without letting her parents know where she was headed? Good looks and getting a *zing* when they touched was not a reason to be so reckless...

Under the glaring lights of the parking lot, Rich could see Vickie's fear about his sudden change in plans. He put a hand on her shoulder, startling her. "I'll never take advantage of you if that's what has you panicked. This is just a side trip. Trust me, all right?"

"Okay."

"And let me go in by myself first. It really is a guy thing."

***

It was only a few miles on the map but a lot longer on the twisting roads and one missed turn that resulted in backtracking. They finally pulled up to the long motor home with a magnetic sign on the side that read 'Doc's Clinic. C. R. M. Strong. Knock before entering.'

"Looks safe enough," Vickie said.

"I'll be back shortly." Rich started to leave the engine running to keep the heater going, then had second thoughts. "I'll take the keys. When you get cold, come on in. That should give me about five minutes of guy to doctor time."

Grrr.

"Hey, we don't have time for growling at each other. Besides, I'd win that one. Still, I don't completely trust you not to take off with my truck. I like you, but you did just sneak out with a hundred-thousand-dollar car a few hours ago."

Grrr.

"Later on that one, lady," he said, then left her in the warm truck. Fuming. Without tunes and nothing but his fleece-lined coat for extra warmth.

Knock. Knock. Knock.

The door opened right away. "Come on in," the good-looking bearded man in his mid-forties said.

The smell of coffee and bacon perfumed the air, the room bright with fluorescent lights and white walls, a desk and three chairs in the living room area rather than a couch. "I'm Chuck. Do you care for some coffee?"

"Rich. And yes, please."

"We're all rich in our own ways," Chuck said with a wink, then poured a cup for the obviously fatigued young man and handed it to him. "Have a seat. Sorry for the pun."

"At least it was a new one. Hey, I hate to bother you so early, but..." Rich sat down and rubbed a hand over his face, trying to figure out how to address the situation.

"So early or late?" Chuck asked while his visitor sought words.

"You called that one right," Rich said. He brought his hand down, looked up and noticed the picture on the desk.

Vickie.

Or her twin. Complete with the cutest ears that stuck out just a smidge.

"Is that your daughter?" Rich asked, picking up the five by seven acrylic frame of a teenage girl holding a twelve-inch long rainbow trout.

"Yes, that's Rhianna Lynn. I took that picture last year. She just turned sixteen yesterday."

Rich's hand went limp and dropped to the table, the photo slipping from his grasp.

"Whoa there, buddy. What's going on?"

Knock. Knock.

Vickie quickly opened the door, not waiting for anyone to answer, her hand covering her eyes. "I'm sorry, I'm sorry. I couldn't wait any longer. It's too cold out there. Are you decent?" she asked, babbling in frustration. Her head turned side to side. "Are you in here, Rich? I don't want to open my eyes in case the doctor's examining you."

"I'm right here, and you can open your eyes... No! Wait a second. Keep them closed."

Rich stood up and led her to a chair. "Sit," he told her, his eyes on Chuck.

"I'm not a dog," she replied sarcastically.

Chuck's eyes widened at hearing her voice. Face obscured by

her hand and head covered with a scarf, the curls that escaped were the same color as Ria's.

"Okay. Open your eyes."

"Tori Lynn?" Chuck asked.

"No. My name is Vickie Lynn Thornwhistle. Who are you?"

The man's face was ashen, his mouth gasping. Vickie could tell he was dumbstruck. "And are you okay? I mean, you're the doctor, right? It looks like *you're* the one who's sick."

"I think he is," Rich said.

"That bacon smells so good," a voice called from the hallway. "Oh, I'm sorry, Dad. I didn't know you had clients this early."

Vickie stood up and faced her doppelganger in gray sweats, her head wrapped in a towel. "*Who* are you?" she asked. *Am I having a dream? A nightmare?*

"Shit! I mean, shoot! Who are *you*?" Rhianna looked at her father, his eyes wide and mouth still agape. "Daddy? Do I have a twin?"

"Sorta," escaped softly, then he took a deep breath and shut his mouth. "And yes, saying shit is appropriate in this case."

"So, who's Ria?" Rich asked, watching Chuck for signs of lying.

"I am," the woman fresh from the shower answered. "Rhianna Lynn Strong."

Vickie noticed the hesitation when her twin said her last name. She was lying about it. Not the time to bring it up, though.

"So, if she's Rhianna Lynn, and I'm Vickie Lynn, who is Tori Lynn?"

Chuck took another deep breath and shook his head. "Me and my big mouth. Shoot."

"No, Daddy," Ria said. "Now's an appropriate time to say shit."

"Shit, shoot, either way, that's why I said sorta. You aren't twins – you're two of triplets. You were all adopted when you were just a few hours old to different parents."

Vickie and Ria stared at each other a moment, then both looked back at Chuck. "So, where's our sister?" Vickie asked.

"And who's our mother?" Ria echoed with the exact same tone and inflection.

"Eerie," Rich said.

"Yeah, right?" added Chuck.

"That's an evasive reply," Ria said. "I'm calling you out on that, as you so often say to me."

"Yeah, I guess I brought you up right."

"Yes, you did. And that's another evasive answer," she said, hands on hips.

"Are Grace and Dusty our parents?" Vickie asked.

"You know them?" Chuck asked.

"That's answering a question with a question," Vickie said. "Yes, Gloria and Roger brought me up right, too," she said, nudging her new-found sister with an elbow of camaraderie.

"Oh, Lord. I knew this day was coming…"

"Hey, Doc. That's more evasiveness. My parents brought me up right, too," Rich said. "Just don't tell me I'm related to them, okay?"

"Unless Dusty and Grace are your parents, no, you're not related." Doc ran his fingers through his long salt and pepper hair. "Why are you here?"

Vickie turned to Rich. "Yeah, why are *you* here? And you never did have a 'guy problem,' did you?"

"You're the only guy problem I have," Rich said. "While you three reconnect, can I go to my truck and get some sleep? I've been driving all night after a full day of family and birthday parties and rescuing damsels in distress and… I just need an hour or two. Please?"

"Ria, show him to the back bedroom and give him an extra blanket. I don't want him passing out. He's too big for me to move around."

"You've moved bigger," Ria said.

"Not without hurting for the next three days," he replied.

"Just saying…"

"Do you two always talk like that?" Vickie asked Chuck.

"Like what?"

"I don't know. Like she's your wife. You're not weird like that, I hope."

"Ew! No!" Chuck said in disgust. "She's my helper here at the clinic. This place isn't much, but it's all we can afford with how much we charge. We don't take insurance, don't have any foundations funding us, and part of my mission is to be mobile. I'm all over the place in this thing. I fix people up, and then I'm on my way."

"Like in Wolf Whistle?" Vickie asked.

"Do you know why they called it that?" Ria barely paused before answering her own question. "It's because the wind blows so hard, it sounds like it's whistling when it blows through the trees and rocks."

"And cracks in the door and window seals," Chuck added. "We left there years ago. How do you know about that?"

"I found an old money order made out to my mother," Vickie said. "What was that all about?"

"She loaned me money. I paid it back. I called that old motorhome we had The Whistler because it was so drafty. Her loan helped me buy this one. It was used but in much better shape and ten feet longer than the previous one. It's not as negotiable in the hills, but we manage to find a place big enough to park for a month. The little towns and hollows are happy to have us around to treat those who need it. We stay put until clients stop showing up."

"So, does that mean Rhianna's homeschooled?"

"You can call me Ria. Yes, I'm homeschooled. Can I ask you a question? Oh, I just did, didn't I? Oops. Another question. What I'm getting at is, are you sick?"

"No," Vickie replied, embarrassed at someone telling her she was inadequate.

"Hey, Dad. Let me take this one. Go finish your coffee and breakfast. I'm giving this beautiful young lady a check-up.

Something's wrong with her and she doesn't even know it."

"But…but…we just met!"

"It's either me or Dad, but one of us is going to find out what's going on in that skinny pasty body. You forget: he and I both know what you *should* look like."

"She's got you there," Chuck said. "She sees herself in the mirror every morning. You may be beautiful, but I agree: you don't look right."

"We're not going back where Rich is, are we?"

"Nope." Ria ushered her to the tiny room on the other side of the office living room combination. "This is my bedroom." She pulled down a cabinet door and revealed a bin of personal belongings, including a pink stuffed unicorn.

Vickie reached up and touched it. "An ooni-corn! I had one almost like it. I was obsessed with them when I was little."

"Really? Me, too!" Ria pulled the animal out and gave it to her. "Hold onto her while I check you out. First, take off your shirt."

"Can I leave on my bra?"

"As long as I don't see anything suspicious, sure. This place is still chilly, even if it isn't as drafty."

Jacket and tee-shirt off, Vickie crossed her arms across her chest and shivered, her bony shoulder bones sharp and angular.

"Geez, woman! You're not much more than a skeleton! Don't your parents feed you?"

"Yeah, they noticed, if that's what you mean. My nanny says I'm too fat. She's bony and thinks I should be, too. If I eat, she makes my life miserable. I swear she has cameras hidden everywhere. If I so much as sneak an olive, she lectures me for an hour on how I'll never get a husband, that fat people have no self-control…"

"Have you told your parents about her?"

Vickie shook her head. "I can't."

"Or won't… So, let me approach this another way. What's the worst that can happen if they fire her?"

"She's already blackmailing them. I just found that out yesterday. Or was that earlier this morning? Anyhow, after my birthday party..." Vickie paused, her eyes glistening in recall of Grace punching Elsa.

"What's wrong? Or what's right?" Ria asked. "Now I know what Dad sees when something's going through my head. What you're feeling is showing on your face."

"Oh, it's right, very right." Vickie grabbed the rainbow afghan from the bed and wrapped it around her shoulders. "Okay, so here's the thing. I was about four when I first met my real mother – our birth mother – but I didn't know who she was. I was never told I was adopted. Everything led me to believe that I was just a late-in-life child. So, one day I kinda got rescued by a woman whose father is my father's – adopted father's – cousin. One thing leads to another, and we're in each other's lives. I sort of get a set of godparents.

"I started suspecting there might be more of a connection when I was thirteen. I confronted Grace – our mom – and she admitted a truth. Not the complete truth, but something she thought would satisfy me. She told me that her mother and my mom – the woman who brought me up – were sisters. None of them got along, so they just ignored each other. That was also her reason why we looked so much alike.

"I didn't get a clue that we were even more closely related until Grace – Mom – punched out Nanny Elsa at my birthday party. She got all wound up when she was slugging it out and referred to me as her daughter. Afterward, she said it was because I was her goddaughter. She tried throwing in a few other smoke and mirrors remarks, but I saw through them. Plus, I saw the shock in her face when she realized that she had claimed me out loud."

"Before I get all distracted with *Mom*..." Ria inhaled deeply with the word, savoring it, then licked her lips, determined not to get distracted. "Why did Mom punch your nanny? I assume Nanny Elsa is your nanny."

Vickie turned her head and showed her the ear that was still itching and burning. "Elsa talked me into getting my ears clipped. This one got infected."

"Ooh. That looks painful. I noticed the difference when I first saw you. I think I should have Dad check that out. So, lie back real quick and let me poke and prod. I think you look so pasty because you're malnourished and fighting an infection."

"Do you know how weird this is?" Vickie asked. "You look and sound just like me. You're not a phantom or a dream." She reached up and touched her arm. "So weird."

"Yeah, I do know, because I get the same feeling. Dad never told me, either." Ria's fingers deftly felt for an enlarged liver or other abnormalities, then satisfied she was in good health, offered her a hand to sit up.

"Yeah… And there's another one of us out there somewhere…" Vickie said dreamily.

"Yeah…" Ria echoed. "Really weird."

"Can I get dressed now?"

"Sure. Hey, let me give you a tank top to wear under everything else. Keeping clothing right next to your skin helps insulate your body heat. After you're dressed, I want Dad to look at that ear."

"Gotcha. Sis."

"Back at ya. Sis."

Both girls shivered in excitement with identical shoulder shrugs, then laughed the same short, "Hah!"

"This is going to be so much fun!" they said at the same time.

"Or not," Vickie groaned. "I still have to go home. I don't live that far away, but I have to go back and make things right for my parents."

"Get dressed, then we'll get Dad to fix you up."

***

Chuck inhaled deeply at seeing the infected wound, resisting the urge to comment on the sloppy work. He stood in front of her and asked, "Have you seen anyone else about this. Other than the person who did the deed?"

"Yeah, Papa Doc cleaned it up last night. He didn't have any lidocaine so let me have a drink of whisky to help numb the pain. How can anyone drink that stuff?"

"They drink it for effect, not flavor. Or so they tell me. Who is this Papa Doc fellow?"

"He's kind of like a grandpa to me. A. B. C. Armstrong is his name. Actually, I have lots of surrogate grandpas. Hal and Silas claim me, too."

Vickie paused her cheery rambling for a moment, then spoke sincerely. "Hey, Chuck. How come you just paled when I said his name?" Vickie looked at Ria and saw a similar reaction. "Okay, you two. Do you know Papa Doc?"

"He does, I never met him," Ria said. "He won't let me. Papa Doc is his father."

"Oh..." Vickie said, then giggled as realization hit. "You sign reads C. R. M. Strong. That's for Chuck Ar-m-strong, am I right?"

"Turn around and let me clean that ear again," Chuck grumbled, then smiled at her cleverness.

"Oh, my God!" Vickie squealed, bouncing up and down in place.

"Hold still," Chuck ordered, his hand on her shoulder. "Which epiphany did you just have?"

"Hal is my grandpa! My honest to goodness biological grandpa. And yours, too, Ria!"

"Took you long enough," Chuck said with a chuckle. "When I'm done, I need to put more topical antibiotics on that. I don't have any antibiotic pills left, so I want you to go back home and tell Papa Doc that your physician in Woodstock said he had confidence that he'll know which one to administer."

"I'm jealous," Ria said with a pout.

"Of what?" Chuck asked.

"She gets to know my grandpa and I don't."

"Both adopted and biological grandpas. And our father and

mother…" Vickie said softly.

"Well, meeting them would be cool, too," Ria said. "I never felt shorted when it came to the parents' aspect of a relationship, but I knew about Papa Doc. I never had a grandfather. Dad, can we go there for a visit? I want to meet him."

"We'll see…"

Ria rolled her eyes at her sister and scowled. *That means no.* A grin bloomed and she raised an eyebrow. *But I have you now. Will you help?*

Face pinched in discomfort as the swab cleaned out the wound, Vickie cut her eyes to the side and gave a discreet thumbs-up. *I got your back, Sis!*

Chapter 6: Eighteenth Birthday

January 4, 2008
9:00 AM

"Hi, Dad. Yeah, I'm okay. I'm sorry I took off with just that lame note. Yes, I did! I wrote it on the whiteboard in the garage. Okay, well, it should still be there. I never thought about you not coming out there to find me. Yeah, well, I also moved the Ghibli. Hey, before you get too wound up, know that I love you and Mom, and the only reason I took off was to see if I could declaw Nanny Elsa. Yeah, well, you might think it's not my job, but she's not only declawed, I think I may have crippled her. No. Wait just a second. Are you sitting down? Okay, then sit down and put me on speakerphone so Mom can hear, too."

Vickie looked over at her audience. Rich had awakened and joined the trio at the table, contentedly gnawing on a piece of bacon between sips of coffee.

"Okay. Here goes. I met my sister. Just one of them, though. Dad? Dad? Is Mom okay? Oh, hi, Mom. Is Dad okay? Yeah, I know that Grace is my bio-Mom and Dusty's my bio-Dad. It doesn't change my love for anyone, though. But hey! I have Ria here. Her name's Rhianna Lynn Armstrong. Say hi, Ria."

Ria rolled her eyes in embarrassment, feeling like a four-year-old on Santa's lap being urged to tell him what she wanted for Christmas. "Hi, Vickie's mom and dad. It's cool to meet her. I didn't know about her, either. No, neither one of us fainted, but Dad got an earful. Yeah, well, say hi to my grandpa, Papa Doc, for me. I hope to meet everyone real soon."

Ria scowled, letting Vickie know she was done talking.

"Yes, Rich is here. He's tanking up on coffee and bacon, getting ready to hit the road back home. We're hoping to miss drivetime traffic. Okay, we'll be careful. Yes, Mom, I always wear my seatbelt. So, don't let Elsa back in the house. She has a ledger loaded with all the stuff she's extorted over the years and from whom. There's a key to her room stuck with tape to the bottom of the drawer in the vase table just outside her room. I don't know if you can legally take it, but at least take pictures of all the pages. I know you shouldn't blackmail her, but it would be so sweet to have her on the other end for a change. Why would you buy her a one-way ticket to Costa Rica? Okay, I'll ask Chuck. Love you! See you by dinner!"

Vickie hit end on the phone. "Wow. That went better than I thought," she said to the group.

Chuck picked up his cup and looked to see how much coffee was left. "They'll probably ground you for life when you get home."

"Only for two years. Or two years less one day. It was worth it! Now, Chuck, tell me about Costa Rica."

"Short answer – and all you ever need to know – is that's where Grace's mother was sent by Hal when he divorced her. You think Nanny Elsa is bad, this woman trumps her. Don't even bring up her name. Pure evil."

Ria glanced at Vickie who glanced back. Rich saw the tacit exchange, missed by the musing Chuck, and jumped in. "Do not ever think about messing with evil, either one of you. Think of it this way: no good can come from it. It will only hurt those you love if you disturb it. Someone else went through hell to get her sent away. Are you seriously wanting to hurt your mothers and Hal by connecting with her?"

"When you put it that way…" Vickie said.

"So, Dad," Ria interjected. "When do we get to meet Tori Lynn? And why do all of us have the same middle name."

"I have no idea why Lynn got stuck in the middle of all of you. Your name choices were by the parents, and none of us knew the other girls' names until later. Actually, nobody else knew Rhianna's middle name until today."

"That's question number two answered," Vickie said. "How about the first one: when do we get to meet Tori Lynn?"

Chuck looked up at Rich. *Help! I'm getting double-teamed!*

"Hey. They're your problems. I'm just the driver," Rich answered, all smiles as he sipped his coffee.

"No, you're not," Vickie said, sidling up to him.

Rich spat out his swallow, choking on it.

Chuck handed him a napkin and waited to make sure he could catch his breath before offering assistance.

"What do you mean?" Rich gasped.

Vickie tried to contain her grin, then gave up. "You're the Sherlock who figured this all out. I just got us headed in the right direction. Sort of."

"I've heard there's a twin thing that goes on," Ria said. "I wonder if there's a triplet thing, too."

"Yup. Gotta be that," Chuck said with a tone of finality. "And that's what you should trust to find Tori. I have to tell you right now, I do not know where she and her parents are."

Ria looked at Vickie and grinned. *Leave it to me. I'll find out her parents' names and let you know. We'll find her yet!*

***

January 3, 2010

18th birthday party

"I'm so nervous," Grace said, holding onto Dusty's arm. "Our little girl is eighteen today. She's going away, I know she is. She hasn't said anything, but I feel it in my bones. She's too young! Too naïve and vulnerable…"

"Like we were?" Dusty asked.

"Oh, Lord…"

"Hey! Don't worry about it. She has four sensible parents now. That's three more than you had. Plus, she has three grandpas. She would have had four if my dad had lived longer, but at least he got to love her as his great-goddaughter when she was four."

"Getting a little moist in here?" Chuck asked, surprising Grace with his first visit in eighteen years.

Grace – very emotional about Vickie turning eighteen and

leaving – had been holding back her tears, but lost control when she saw him. She smacked him once on the arm. "Chuck? Why did you do that?" she hissed. "Why did you…you." Then she started blubbering, pounding on him, swinging uncontrollably, an emotional explosion of frustration, rage, and sorrow.

Chuck hadn't known what to expect after all these years and was prepared for anything. Keeping her at arm's length to stop more punches, he stared at how beautiful she still was, shaking his head at how her impetuousness hadn't faded. "I tried to talk you out of it dozens of times but you signed those papers. Twice. If it wasn't for me, you'd have lost contact with these girls forever."

Suddenly, she was helpless and remorseful, seeking comfort in his arms, rocking back and forth in his brotherly hug, still full of guilt at her poor decision but grateful that he had found a way to make it work for both of them.

Dusty looked at the handsome man holding his wife. "I don't think we've been introduced. I'm Dusty Rhodes, husband, father…"

"Counselor, comforter, and probably cook when needed," Chuck continued, then bent down and kissed Grace on the top of the head. "It's okay," he told her. "But I really *don't* know where the third one is…"

"Third one?" Grace and Dusty screeched, Grace pulling out of the embrace.

"Oops. You didn't tell her?" Chuck asked, looking into the hallway at Vickie.

"Nope. Mom and Dad – Gloria and Roger – and I decided not to. For a long time, Grace thought she'd lost twins. And then she found out that they were alive and adopted out and…

Vickie looked into the hallway and gave the hand signal to come in. "Well, surprise, Grace and Dusty!" She wrapped her arm around Ria's waist. "You'll have to be happy with just having the two of us around for a while. Even Chuck doesn't know where Tori is."

"Hi, I'm Rhianna Lynn Armstrong. I think you know my dad,

Chuck, and grandpa, Papa Doc." She frowned at her father. "At least, the way you two were hugging, I hope you know him."

"I know Papa Doc," Dusty said, "but I just met Chuck. I heard about him, how he kept her alive and sane while pregnant." He took a deep breath. "Thank God she never said anything negative about him or *I* would have been the one punching him."

"Hey, girls!" Rich said, coming in with a fistful of gift bags in hand, oblivious of the excitement that had just transpired. "Long time, no see," he said to Vickie with an eye roll.

Vickie let go of her sister and nudged him, shoulder-to-shoulder, giving him a quick 'shush.'

"I'll pretend I didn't see that," Grace said, then did her own eye roll.

"Tori?" Dusty asked, trying to bring the conversation back to his being the father of triplets.

"Tori Lynn," Ria said. "Dad won't tell us her last name or the name of her parents. He's the best secret-keeper in the world." She pointed to herself. "I'm living proof of that. Don't worry, Dusty. We'll find Tori and let you and Grace know where she is."

"Yeah! We'll let you two know first!" Vickie said, her index finger held up to emphasize the number one priority.

Rich paled, Chuck and Ria gasped, and Grace and Dusty growled.

"What?" Vickie asked, bringing her hand down, looking around the room for the cause of the mixed emotions. When everyone's eyes followed her hand, she realized she had forgotten to take off her engagement ring.

"Oh, shoot!" she moaned.

"Nope," Ria said. "That one's worthy of an 'oh, shit!'"

"Rich…" Dusty said menacingly, his eyes narrowed as he tried to take his wife's restraining hand off him, ready to pummel the fiancé.

"Dusty! Don't hit him!" Vickie blurted out. "I just got it this morning. We haven't done anything stupid. We were going to announce it tonight. He wanted to give it to me in front of everyone. Come on, you and Grace were practically married when you were eighteen. At least, he's older and has a college degree, almost his masters."

Dusty relaxed and Grace started giggling, remembering their first night together, of innocence lost on the couch, the floor, the pool table... Then she remembered being caught by her mother the morning after. Suddenly, she sobered up, recalling the gut punches and threats of false charges that had robbed her of her daughters and precious time with Dusty, of being shot point-blank by the woman who had birthed her, thankfully now exiled to Costa Rica.

She took a deep breath to compose herself. "Are you two 'practically married'?" she asked, using her daughter's euphemism for sexually active.

"No," Vickie said. "I wish we were, but he said no."

Dusty clapped his hand on Rich's shoulder, a little harder than a friendship smack, a firm reminder that Vickie was still his little girl and not some floozy. "I guess I can thank you for that," he said, then whispered, "You have more restraint than I had. Three babies resulted. Remember that. Very fertile women. At least, the first time around."

"So, do I have your blessing? I mean, I've got another set of parents to ask, but it might go easier with Gloria and Roger if you've already given the go-ahead."

"Do you think we could stop them?" Dusty asked Grace.

"Not a chance in hell. Do you think he's worthy?" she asked him.

"He's been hanging around her like a dog at a butcher shop, not even stealing scraps, waiting for her to turn eighteen. He's got a career chosen thanks to Chuck's influence. Yup. I think the two of them will make a good team. Lord, I hope they don't have babies too soon."

"Why not?" she asked.

"I'm only thirty-seven! I'm too young to be a grandpa!

However, a little IVF procedure and you could have another one."

Grace squeezed his arm and pulled him close. "Or two or three. I think I'm ready."

Chapter 7: Blue Collar Wedding

January 23, 2010

"I have a little information you might be interested in," Silas said, setting his laptop on the coffee table.

"Anything to distract me from thinking about my little girl getting married next week," Roger said. "Why is she in such a big hurry?"

Silas looked down his nose. "Well, if she really isn't saving herself for that young man, he's sure doing a good job of making it look like she is. That boy has got to have the bluest balls on the east coast. Not that I checked, but he sure looks frustrated to me!"

Roger shook his head, not wanting to think about the testicles of the man his daughter would be marrying. "What kind of info do you have?"

Knock! Knock!

Roger got up and answered the door. "Hal, Grace, Dusty! Come on in. Silas was just going to have a little chit chat with me. We can finish later. What's going on?"

"Actually," Silas said, "I wanted them here, too. We're going to have a little video conference call if you don't mind."

"Don't mind at all. Should I call Gloria?"

"He already did," Gloria said, coming in with a tray loaded with canapés. She set them on the counter of the wet bar. "The bar's always open here, so help yourselves or tell me what you want."

"I want to know what's going on," Roger said, his voice edged in frustration.

Silas opened his laptop and turned it around so everyone could see it. "Does anyone recognize her?"

"That's the bitch who ditched Grace just hours after she had the babies!" Dusty growled. "Dumped her incoherent and disoriented at that so-called recovery house, left her there to freeze. If Chuck hadn't told us where she'd be..." He grunted in a feral rage, too angry to continue.

The little inset window at the bottom corner of the computer screen suddenly became active as Chuck came into view. "That's Ellen, one of the two neo-natal nurses who were there when Grace delivered. I didn't know until just now that she was the one who moved Grace to recovery. I'm pretty sure she's the one who gave Dr. Buddy the heads up that the FBI was on its way, giving him the chance to escape. The other nurse came with me and stayed around for a few years, helping me with Ria and getting the mobile clinic started."

"Okay, Chuck – and only Chuck – do you know who this is?" Silas asked.

"Nope. Never saw her," he said, then leaned closer to the monitor to look at the angry faces on the gathering of family and friends on the other side. "Should I know her?" he asked.

"That's Elsa," Roger hissed. "Vickie's nanny. For twelve years, she extorted thousands of dollars both in cash and goods from us. Two years ago, she slipped away from the hospital after she caught wind that she might have been found out."

"And," Silas said, keying in another picture on the monitor, "the same person known as Ellen Nyman; neo-natal specialist from Finland."

"Who are they?" Grace asked, looking at the side-by-side photos.

"One and the same person. These are her before and after pictures from the clinic where she got a nose job and a stomach staple. It seems she had a lot of dirt on quite a few people. She went around the country, working for black market baby doctors and white slavery mommy manipulators like Dr. Buddy. She'd collect information on the clients who adopted the infants, particularly those who claimed the children as their own biological babies, then blackmailed the parents for money to get a new body. Heck of a way to improve oneself," Silas said. "One blackmail after another; one tummy tuck or nose job, and then it's onto the next sucker."

"Until she couldn't get any skinnier," Roger said, "so then she started amassing material goods. Well, you've solved another one, Sherlock…er…Silas."

"I only have one dilemma left," Silas said. "I've contacted everyone in that ledger Elsa Ellen Nyman left behind. Some of the folks were happy to get the goods back, a few didn't want any part of them because they didn't want to remember that part of their lives, but most of the folks had filed with their insurance companies and already been compensated. They couldn't take the material goods back, so they said to just donate them to a good charity. That's where the dilemma comes in."

"You don't know which one to give it to?" Roger asked.

"Nope, I do. I was thinking about calling it Thrive," Silas said. "My dilemma is trying to figure out if I should have Chuck run it or give it to the girls."

"Heck ya, give it to the girls!" Chuck said via internet connection. "I have enough on my plate as it is."

"Which girls?" Hal asked.

"Don't know, don't care," Chuck said, "as long as it isn't me. Oh, were you asking me or Silas, Hal?"

"Anyone," Hal said, "but probably Silas since this is his idea."

"All of them," Silas said. "Gloria is already connected with lots of charities and knows the ins and outs of non-profits. Grace has been running back and forth between at least a dozen foundations, fighting white slavery and establishing recovery houses. And all the young girls – or both Vickie and Ria – have always had that nurturing, helping others bend. I just want to make sure that when we finally find Tori Lynn Whatever-Her-Last-Name is, she'll have a place to come if she has that same passion, too."

"All those in favor say, 'Aye.'" Roger asked.

Everyone said, "Aye."

"And then they all Thrived…" Chuck said. "I gotta scoot. I have someone waiting for me in the other room. I promise that Ria and I will be there next week for the wedding. We still haven't got a gift.

Any suggestions?"

"Just yourselves. The young couple insists that it's a low-key event. For some reason, the groom and groomsmen are all wearing denim and fleece; the ladies, bright tees and flannels," Grace said.

"Except for the bride. Vickie said that wearing a white traditional gown was her gift to her mother," Dusty added.

"Probably the only bride in this family in generations who deserved it," Roger said. "Not that I'm complaining."

"Shush," Silas said. "Too much information."

"We'll figure something out for them," Chuck said. "Later!"

Silas closed the laptop and looked over at Roger. "Do you think he'd be so easy going if it was Ria getting married?"

"His day is coming, I'm sure," Roger said. "Maybe sooner than he thinks."

***

January 30, 2010

"I'm so nervous," Gloria said, her hands fidgeting with the corsage sitting in front of her. "I can't put this on myself!"

"No one's asking you, too," Grace said. "Let me help."

Grace picked up the single orchid surrounded with white violets; white on white flowers set on a gathered white lace background. She set her hand under Gloria's lapel and pinned the corsage on. "You know, I really think this is perfect. Yes, it's simple, yet elegant. Just like Vickie. She never needed all the bling. We both know it made her uncomfortable. She always rebelled, saying, 'Diamonds aren't for everyone.' But you know what? She's the diamond. Tough, simple, sharp…"

"Tough enough to cut through steel and determined enough to do it if needed. Yes, Grace, we brought up a great girl."

"I'm just glad you let me in her life!"

"And I'm glad you gave her life! My goodness, I don't know what we would have done if you had contested the adoption and tried to get her back. A simple DNA test would have proved you were her mother, and we didn't have any documentation. Do you know how much I feared she'd send off for one of those DNA kits and find out that Roger and I weren't her real parents?"

"But you *were* her real parents," Grace said. "Blood doesn't make a parent. Good grief, look at Victoria! She's my blood mother and horrid! She's your sister, but you two couldn't be more different. You may be my biological aunt, but I feel like *you're* my sister. If I could 'un-mother' her, I would."

"Yes, and as soon as Vickie met you, she fell in love with you. She loved you for you, not because she was obligated by genetics. Blood meant nothing to her then and now. Love means everything and I know that."

"Yup, and that's why she's getting married today. I'm glad you and Roger are letting her. Those two just seem right together. I'm sure they'll have a wonderful life, pursuing their dream."

***

"Oh, my God! I thought Chuck was going to pass out when you punked him, coming out in my dress."

"He really did believe me for a minute there," Ria said, changing back into her casual maid of honor outfit – a denim skirt, leather boots, and white tank top with a red plaid shirt over it.

"Who was that guy you brought to play your intended?" Vickie asked. "He's kind of cute."

"No, he's an absolute doll! I thought you met him before, though. He was with me for a while at the rehearsal dinner."

"No, I was late, remember?" Vickie turned her back to Ria. "Can you zip this for me?"

Ria pushed the veil train aside and zipped her in. "Yeah, what was that all about? Late to your own wedding rehearsal dinner? I thought I was going to have to dash out and come back in and fake being you again."

"Again? You've done it before?" Vickie asked, turning around to give her the evil eye, then laughing at her own joke. "Yeah, I tried it three times but only got away with it once. It'd be easier if we lived closer. Now if the folks are suspicious, they look up to see if

I'm wearing a hat or have my hair down. Kind of hard to fake the ears."

"Easier for you than me," Ria said. "You can stuff a wad of modeling clay behind each one to make them stick out. Taping mine back is a little more obvious." Ria held her ear back with one finger, checking the effect. "Do you think I should get my ears done?"

"Don't you dare! I know it's your body and all that, but you're perfect just the way you are. Don't let anyone else's idea of beauty make you change you, all right?"

"All right," Ria said. "Now, hair up or down?" she asked, lifting her loose curls.

"Let's go for the elegant country: hair up with denim and red flannel. Show off those angel ears!"

"So, why were you late to your own rehearsal. Were you and Rich finally getting it on?"

"Ria!"

"Ah, that's an evasive reply. I'll take that as a yes. Watch it. Grace said she got pregnant the first time."

Vickie blushed, lips pursed in frustration, wanting to deny what her sister suspected but knowing it was no use. She blew out her held breath. "Don't tell anyone, please."

"Duh! It's nobody's business, including mine. Two days early is close enough. You still deserve to wear white."

"What about you, Ria? The hunk? Are you two 'getting it on'?"

"Eet!" Ria made a noise like a penalty buzzer. "Not your business!"

"So, you're not blushing or mad at me for suggesting it which means you're not doing anything, but you'd like to be. I know I've never met him, but he looks familiar."

"Don't concern yourself with us. You're the one getting married in," Ria looked up at the clock, "fifteen minutes. Where are the moms?" she asked, walking through the doorway to look down the hall.

"Oooh! You said, 'Don't concern yourself with *us*,' not me.

96

More serious than you want anyone but me to know about. Don't worry, my lips are sealed."

Ria quickly looked back at Vickie and said, "Shush!" then left.

A moment later, three women came in. "Oh, here you are!" Gloria said, following Ria back into the room, Grace beside her. "We were looking all over the place for you. I still think we should have had the wedding at the Club. At least, I wouldn't have gotten lost." Gloria fanned herself with the announcement. "I'm sorry, dear. Danged hot flashes make me moody. This is your day. Really, if this is where you want to have your wedding, it's fine with us. All of us."

"I hope so since it's almost time. Grace, would you help me with this makeup? I can't get this eyeliner straight and I know Mom can't see up close."

"Oh, I feel so inadequate," Gloria moaned.

"Why don't you help me with my hair?" Ria asked. "I can't see the back of my head and want to make sure I don't have a flat spot. Can you do that for me?"

"Oh, yes, dear. I'm so glad you and Chuck could come. Where is he?"

"I think he met a new old friend. They're getting reacquainted," Ria said.

"Man, I wish he'd get a boyfriend," Grace said. "He's been alone for way too long."

"A boyfriend?" Gloria gasped. "He's gay?"

"Well, duh!" Ria said. "Do you think Dusty would let a straight man hug on Grace like that?"

"Well, I don't know..." Gloria bent back to picking up the curls in Ria's hair and pinning them in place. "I guess it doesn't make any difference," she said.

"I know he goes on dates occasionally, claiming he's 'going out with the guys.' But I've seen the way some men check him out. Women, too, but he never returns their looks. He is the epitome of discretion. I don't think he knows that I know. I tried to bring it up once and he got so flustered and embarrassed, I decided that it really wasn't any of my business. As soon as I'm ready to go out on my own, he can do his own thing, find his Mr. Right, or at least look around for him."

"Wow! That's pretty sensitive," Grace said, sitting back in the chair, overwhelmed with emotions.

"Brought up by a gay dad who is also a non-profit physician," Ria said. "Of course, I'm sensitive! Okay, are we about done here? I'm not wearing any makeup because as the sensitive person that I am, I'll be crying before Vickie takes her first step down the aisle. *Sniff, sniff.* See what I mean?"

Gloria opened her purse and handed Ria an embroidered handkerchief. "Here you go, honey. You can keep it. I packed at least a dozen of them."

"That's a good thing," Grace said, plucking one of them out of her friend's Coach bag, using it to dab under her nose. "I'm glad you planned ahead."

"Everyone decent?" Roger called into the room. "They're ready for us."

All eyes looked at Vickie and grinned.

"Last chance to back out," Roger teased. He suddenly became serious when he noticed his daughter was pale and blinking back tears. He moved in close and held her tight. "Because if you don't want to do this, it's not too late. Anything you decide is fine with us. No one will think less of you…"

Vickie reached up and stilled him with a soft hand to his chest. "I'm fine, Daddy. You're not losing me. You're gaining a son. I never heard you wish you had had one, but you're getting one anyhow. All right?"

Roger nodded and sniffed, then stepped back and took a handkerchief from the inside of his jacket to stifle his liquid emotions.

"Okay. I'm ready," Vickie said. She looked around the room. "All noses wiped and tears erased? I hope so because I'm ready to become Mrs. Richard Rickman the Third!"

Ria lined up the ladies in the order they were entering, making sure all the men were ready to escort the women. "Where's my dad?" she whispered to Grace.

"He dashed out of here before we came to see you. He said he had to go get Vickie's present. What did he get her?"

"Danged if I know. He's back to being Mr. Mysterious again."

Hal stood at the front of the line, waiting for the others to make last-minute adjustments, anxious at standing so close to his college sweetheart without her husband at her side. Finding a trickle of courage to make a joke, he whispered to Gloria, "I always knew I'd be escorting you down the aisle someday," and subconsciously added a flirtatious wink.

She lightly slapped his hand. "That was eons ago," she whispered harshly but with a tint of levity. She switched it to sincerity. "I'm not sorry Victoria messed everything up between us, though, because I wound up with Roger. But I do regret her latching her claws into you."

"Yeah, well she was one vicious tigress. It took me years to get her off my back, but I managed it." He watched her face carefully and added, "At least I got Grace out of it."

She flushed suddenly, her gloved hand up to fan her face. "Damned hot flashes," she hissed.

Hal grabbed one of the flyers from the table next to them and offered it to her. "So, are my suspicions true?" he asked. "Victoria had others besides me?"

"As you have said many times, the only good you ever got out of my sister was Grace. Let's leave it at that. Blood isn't everything, right?" she asked, then fixed him with a stare that said, 'Drop it!'

Hal took a deep breath and groaned. "You're right."

The electronic keyboard in the hall started playing Mendelssohn's Wedding March, stopping any further discussion on the subject of Grace's paternity. Gloria looked over at Hal, moistness reddening his eyes. "Your granddaughter – my daughter –

is getting married in a minute. Pull it together, Hal. You got this."

He looked at her and patted her hand again. "Yeah, *I do*. Come on, Mom. Let's go hear them share *their* I do's."

***

"I, Richard Othello Albert Rickman the Third, promise to love, cherish, and work through any disagreements with my spouse, through sickness and health, poverty and wealth, whether we're near or miles apart. You are and always will be my mate for life. Swans have nothing on us, Vickie Lynn Thornwhistle."

"I, Vickie Lynn Thornwhistle, promise to be your best friend, confidant, dedicated lover, mother to your children, helpmate, and coworker, and even cook and mend for you, wherever we may be, whatever our financial or health circumstances, forever and ever, amen."

"By the power invested in me by the Commonwealth of Massachusetts, I now pronounce you husband and wife," Silas said. He looked up to the audience, scanning for the one missing member of his adopted family – Chuck. He spotted him, grinning at the late arrival when he saw the three people he had brought with him. "Ladies and gentlemen, I present to you, Mr. and Mrs. Richard Rickman the Third!"

Rather than bend to kiss her, Rich stepped back, took a deep breath, then gave a graduate-level lion's roar. Loud and long, he embellished his performance with arms waving in the air before ending with a gasp and a huge smile.

The audience clapped, hooted, and whistled at his display of victory.

Vickie Lynn stepped forward and brought her hands up, then lowered them slowly, indicating she wanted everyone to calm down. "Now, as everyone knows, it's the lioness who actually does the hunting, making sure her mate is well-fed and safe from predators." She took a deep breath, looked around to make sure she had everyone's attention, then gave her own resounding roar, eliciting even more cheers, whistles, and foot stomps.

When she was finished with her loud feline claim, Rich pulled her close and looked her in the eye, letting her catch her breath for what was coming next. "Come here, wife. There's nothing in this world we can't conquer together."

The two embraced and kissed to more cheers and tears. Even Silas shed a few dribbles of liquid happiness before the couple finally broke apart. "To the banquet room, everyone!" he said. "Line up to kiss the bride, then it's cake and champagne!"

"Are you sure we should have come, Luther?" Leanne whispered from the back row, catching glimpses of the newlywed couple over and between the shoulders of the guests, trying to watch the proceedings without being seen. "I mean, we didn't even get an invitation."

"Are you kidding? We got a second-hand verbal and that's good enough for me. Plus, if Gloria would have known where to send the invite, I'm sure she would have. You've been wanting to see the other girls for over eighteen years, and now you're wanting to leave? Not a snowball's chance in the Sahara for that one. Look at Tori."

Tori Lynn Greene, huddled in-between coats and sweaters hanging from the hooks on the wall, was sneaking a glimpse of the guests, then pulling jacket sleeves back to disappear into the fabric and fur. *Why did we have to come here? Who are these people they want me to meet? I want to go home...*

The End of Diamonds Aren't for Everyone: Vickie's Story
Book Two of Triplets: Three Aren't One

Afterword

I'm not leaving out anyone in this series, **Triplets: Three Aren't One**. Tori Lynn just takes a bit longer to get to know folks. She, Vickie and Rhianna, Chuck, Grace and Dusty, and all those wannabe grandpas and everyone else in the family will be back very soon.

Here's a quick overview of the stories in the series:

Grace – Surviving an evil mother was just the first of her challenges. A gritty women's fiction story. *The Set Up*

Vickie – Gloria and Roger's daughter – is dealing with lifestyles of the rich and famous in *Diamonds Aren't for Everyone*

Ria – Brought up in the backwoods by a single father dedicated to helping those less fortunate, she also has *That Magic Touch.* Is there more to life than healing and living on the edge? Would Evan be the one to show her what made life bright and enjoyable?

Tori – An independent free thinker brought up by hippie parents who grow wine grapes and pot, Tori tries not to fall in love with the new hand with the sexy voice in *How Love Grows.*

Silas – Everyone's friend, confidant, and go-to guy in this series, has a secret. Find out more about him in *They Call Me Sherlock.*

About the Author

Author Dani Haviland started writing late in life and has been making up for lost time with a flood of works from sports, rom-coms, historicals, time travel, and Sweet and Sassy romances to Unforgettable romantic suspense and cozy mystery tales – with a few short stories thrown in to round out the reading experience.

Dani is also the owner of Chill Out! Books, one of the publishers for The Authors' Billboard. Follow her on Amazon and BookBub to make sure you get her latest stories.

Contact information:

Website: www.danihaviland.com

Facebook: Dani Haviland Author and Dani Haviland & Friends

Readers Group: http://bit.ly/2DaniStTeam

BookBub: http://bit.ly/BBDani

Goodreads: http://bit.ly/2DHgdrds

Email: dani@danihaviland.com

Twitter: @dani_haviland and @gr8authors

I love to hear from readers!

Sign up for my newsletter to get the latest information on new releases, free stuff, and contests at: http://bit.ly/2DHnews

Other Books by Dani Haviland

ARLIE UNDERCOVER SERIES
(romantic suspense based in Alaska and Arizona)

A Stingray Christmas: (Book One) Anchorage detective on medical leave travels from Alaska to Arizona to see for the first time the son he'd fathered as an anonymous sperm donor. Great and rotten surprises await the cop with the smartest smartphone around.

The Biggest Heart Ever: (Book Two) When would Arlie learn that trying to do everything by himself could be deadly—and make Charlene a widow before they were married?

Always a Bigger Fish: (Book Three) Back in Alaska, Arlie finds out he's a target. Will vacationing detective Billy Burke (from THE FAIRIES SAGA) have information to help nab the scalper?

How to Fix a Broken Life: (Book Four) When Arlie's very pregnant wife is kidnapped by pseudo terrorists, will he be the one to rescue her or will a surprise hero come in to save the day?

Because You Said So: (Book Five) Something's amiss at the Port of Anchorage. Will Arlie be able to solve it and still be back in time to wear the Santa suit?

Heaven and Heartbreak: (Book Six) How will Louie handle being a daddy? And what about that baby momma?

TRIPLETS: THREE AREN'T ONE

The Set Up: (Book One) Grace's story. How it all began with the mother from hell.

Diamonds Aren't for Everyone: (Book Two) Vickie's story – Growing up a billionaire.

That Magic Touch: (Book Three) Ria's story – Doctoring in the backwoods with secrets.

How Love Grows: (Book Four) Tori's story – Growing up in vineyards and marijuana farms.

They Call Me Sherlock: (Book Five) – Back to Woodstock with a friend.

THE FAIRIES SAGA SERIES
(historical fiction/time travel, listed in order):

Kibbles and Bits: FREE ebook: Sample the first stories in the series before you buy. The Fairies Saga stories. Find out how the first five books got their crazy names, too.

Naked in the Winter Wind: (Book One) How does an older woman wind up as a young hottie in Revolutionary War era North Carolina? First book in the time travel series.

Ha'Penny Jenny: (Book Two) More about the naïve and psychic young girl who was adopted into a time traveling family. Will her past catch up to her?

Aye, I am a Fairy: (Book Three) Young British lord finds himself entwined with a time traveling family and must decide if he should go back in time, too.

Dances Naked: (Book Four) Directionally challenged time traveler is rescued by Cherokee in 18th century. What must he do before the chief will show him to The Trees, the portal through time?

Chasing Christmas: (Book Five) A young Cherokee is rescued from an abusive man and changes the lives of many in this 18th century America family.

The Great Big Fairy: (Book Six) Very tall Benji grew up in the 20th century but was born in the 18th. When he finds a way to return to his grandparents in the distant past, he goes for it. Once there, he realizes he can't stay, but must return to the future.

Little Bear and the Ladies: (Book Seven) What's a bachelor trapper to do with all the females he rescues from the Hessian mercenaries? He'd better hurry and figure something!

Little Drummer Boy: (Book Eight) Young Scout works to earn money for a home in post-Revolutionary War America but runs up against prejudices and snowstorms.

Never Too Young: (Book Nine) Scout and Ha'Penny Jenny have grown up, but will they be able to spend their life together, or will the past and ruffians get in their way?

Time in a Little Blue Bottle: (Book Ten) Elvis, Mark Twain, and the prime vampire are racing to get the bottle of Fountain of Youth water before sweet Bella and the youthful pickpocket. So why are time travelers Marty Melbourne and Master Simon interested?

Kidnapped!: (Book Eleven) Benji's sister has been abducted and he and his Scottish police officer brother-in-law will do anything to get her back...even trust the mysterious letter sent by an ancestor, a convict on The First Fleet into Australia!

Big Mac: (Book Twelve) Can Big Mac stop his sire, the errant Viking time traveler, from starting a pandemic?

BENJI, THE LOST YEARS
(contemporary novellas about a young Benji MacKay)

Pool Boy Wanted: No Experience Preferred: (rather racy) Young Benji has been a hostage and slave, but life gets worse when an older woman decides she wants him as her own.

Luke the Unexpected: Love of classic motorcycles brought them together, but Luke and Holly have other challenges to face. Find out how their friend Benji got his stripes here.

STAND ALONE NOVELLAS
(contemporary romances)

Kit Kringle: An Alaskan Tale: Kay moved to Alaska for the wrong reasons, then decided to stay and start her own business. What she hadn't planned on were prejudices and falling in love.

Be My Angel: Wyatt's dream to help save the wild mustangs began with the purchase of a rundown ranch in western Oregon. What he hadn't anticipated was being mesmerized by a sassy woman in a wheelchair.

Three Are One: The post chaplain tried to help the young widow adjust, but would his feelings for her and the search for his lost sister cause problems?

One Arctic Summer: That unforgettable summer of 1994 in Barrow, Alaska, and the touch she never forgot…If she goes back, will he remember her?

The Polar Xpress: Will the California chiropractor get a first chance at romance with the owner of Second Chance Kennels when he is stranded in Alaska?

Too Fast For You: Ten years after Little League, two talented professional baseball players wind up on the same minor league team. Will she remember him? And will their friendship be ruined if she does?

www.ingramcontent.com/pod-product-compliance
Lightning Source LLC
Chambersburg PA
CBHW061256170626
46809CB00007B/3012

* 9 7 8 1 9 4 6 7 5 2 8 4 0 *